FOOLED BY SO-CALLED LOVE

An Anthology by

Laconia Renee, Sparkle Lewis, Christina Fletcher, Cabria, Marcy and Rachal Perez

Domestic violence (also called intimate partner violence (IPV), domestic abuse or relationship abuse) is a pattern of behaviors used by one partner to maintain power and control over another partner in an intimate relationship.

Domestic violence does not discriminate. Anyone of any race, age, sexual orientation, religion or gender can be a victim – or perpetrator – of domestic violence. It can happen to people who are married, living together or who are dating. It affects people of all socioeconomic backgrounds and education levels.

For those who have been affected by relationship abuse, those who are currently in abusive relationships, and those who are working to heal, call the National Domestic Violence Hotline:

1-800-799-7233

To submit a manuscript for our review,

email us at

submissions@majorkeypublishing.com

By His Mighty Hand

By Laconia Reneé

CHAPTER ONE

Sasha moved around the house so effortlessly yet shaking while getting Charlie's things together before he went to work. Her early mornings consisted of the same routine, if not for one or two events changing, according to Charlie's attitude. The morning's sun shone on his strewn pair of jeans in front of the couch, showing Sasha that she had forgotten an article of clothing that he'd climbed out of during his drunken stumble into the house in the late of night.

Hurriedly, she scurried over to them to pull them off the floor, because Charlie would complain about how horrible the home looked if the floor wasn't spotless. A single condom wrapper slipped out of the back pocket, landing on the floor. Her eyes immediately darted over to it and squinted for a moment to calculate that it had in fact happened. She could clearly see that it had been torn and that there was not a condom inside. Sasha's tears pooled her eyes with her throat squeezing. He'd done it again. He had gotten so drunk as to touch another female the way he was supposed to be touching her.

The only thing to pull her out of her world of hurt was their screaming son. She gasped and flinched at his wail, hurrying to his call with her boyfriend's coat, shirt, shoes, and his jeans still in her hands. She only dumped them in the rocking chair inside her son's bedroom to get him out of his bed, and to sit and rock with him.

"What the fuck?" she heard from the doorway.

Clutching six-year-old Dean in her arms, she rocked back and forth with her bottom lip caged between her teeth. Sasha was barely keeping it together as it was, let alone having Charlie to scold her because of their special needs son having a bad dream.

Charlie took his wide, tattooed hand down his face and frowned at her animatedly. "Shut him the fuck up, Sasha," he demanded in a baritone that made her flinch. "I'm not fuckin' playin' with you. I got shit to do, so I need my sleep. You already half-ass everything around here. Don't half-ass this."

Her lips parted. Before she could get anything out, she decided that it was best to hold it.

"You want to say something?" he pressed, taking a few steps into the room.

Sasha wondered how his once rock-hard build when he was dressed in nothing but his boxers would turn her on. Now, he frightened her and made her sick to her stomach.

"Say what's on your heart, Sasha."

She looked down at Dean's forehead, kissed it, and rocked a little harder while keeping in all of the things she wanted to say.

Purposely, Charlie punched the pane of the door to make her jump a little, then exited the room for the rest of the sleep that he claimed he needed. One would think that he would've stayed where he was, the night prior, after going round-for-round with one of Sasha's co-workers.

It took her all of ten minutes to sit with her son until he realized he wasn't inside his nightmare anymore, run his bathwater, then help him into the tub so she could get the laundry and breakfast started.

Since it was her day off, all she had to do was get Charlie's breakfast prepared and take Dean to school. The summer was vastly approaching, and she had yet to pull together a schedule for him. Sasha knew that she was slipping. Sleep deprivation wasn't helping on that front. She would stay awake and try to wait for Charlie to come home so she could be the woman he claimed to have remembered.

Bending down inside the refrigerator, she placed a carton of eggs back inside as she blew a hard stream of breath through her lips. She realized that she needed terribly to go grocery shopping. There were only two eggs left inside the carton that she had put back. As soon as she stood and turned around, a heavy hand caught the side of her cheek. The impact was so grand that it busted a pocket of blood in her jaw, which splattered across the wall closest to her. Sasha hit the floor with her back, hard, causing a thudding sound to thunder throughout the kitchen.

Charlie stood over her with his jeans in his hand.

Sasha trembled with her hand against her cheek. Her eyes were wide and cloudy, trying to figure out what she had done to deserve his hand this morning.

"Bitch, you went through my pants?" he asked through a hiss.

9

Viciously, she shook her head to deny it.

"Don't you lie to me. Where the fuck is my wallet?"

"On-on-on the dresser," she stammered. "It fell out, so I put it where you would see it."

"Well, I *didn't* see it!" he roared. "Let me find out that you took anything out of that motherfucker, and I promise you that I'm mailing pieces of you back to your hoe ass mama."

With hurt-filled eyes, she watched him as he had stepped over her and rounded the corner. Once picking herself up off the floor, she could hear him on the phone, yet she hadn't known who he was speaking with. A knife in the sink had gotten her attention over his conversation. Many moments, like this one, she only daydreamed of swiping it across her wrist to end all things and to make Charlie suffer a meaningless life as a single father, yet she didn't want to leave Dean all alone.

Nobody wanted to be caged. The wind blowing across Flex's light-colored face was like heaven. He wasn't in the yard, and he wasn't doing an inmate transfer. Finally, he was free. He took a moment to take his deep, emerald colored eyes up to each tower on either side of him, to remind himself that he would never set foot inside the walls of a prison again.

A car rode up the hill on his right, kicking up dust behind it. He reached inside the bag he carried that had been full of his belongings that he had arrived in and grabbed a steel lighter out of it. A black 1965 Ford Mustang with a showroom finish stopped a few feet away from him, just as he flicked his lighter. Then, a young woman stepped out dressed in a pair of cut-off denim shorts, suffocating tank top, and a pair of black thigh-high boots. She gave him a smile that was similar to his own as she tossed him the keys.

Flex dropped his bag and caught the keys. He wasn't prepared to catch the woman's 150 pounds in his arms. Sincere wrapped her arms around her brother's neck, finally letting out a round of tears that she had been holding in for the past eight years.

"This has got to be a dream," he whispered.

She pulled back, fingering her wavy strands away from

her face. "Why would you say that?"

"Because your mean ass is crying." He chuckled.

"Shut up," she said with a giggle, on the heel of a sniffle. "Come. Your kingdom awaits."

Flex picked up his bag before his sister could drag him away from it. "Where'd you get the whip?"

"Got it at an auction last week. Granddaddy took me."

"Old Dad, huh? He doesn't even like cars like that."

"But he knew you did, so he wanted to be a part of it." Sincere opened her own door, dropping her weight inside the passenger's seat. "Speaking of Old Dad… he's still upset at you for doing this bid."

Flex threw his bag into the back seat and sat inside the driver's seat with a grin. "Daddy will get over it. It was something I had to do to get the police off his ass."

"Well, you better play it safe this time because not having you out there almost drove me insane."

"Sin?"

"Yes?" Easily, she slipped on her aviator shades before looking at her older brother by three years.

"How's my throne looking?"

12

"Empty as hell. Waiting for the king to return to it."

"Good. Good."

CHAPTER TWO

Sasha pinned up her hair and stared in the mirror inside the locker room. Her boss had a strict policy for flawless, believable makeup, and remaining in shape. Though she was only a waitress at the cabaret where she worked, she still had to keep her hourglass frame in check and her face as pretty as it could be. Thankfully, after she had gotten herself together at home, she kept ice against her face and was able to cover her bruise with concealer.

She tightened her high ponytail and ran her hand over her bangs before leaving. Her jersey top that had her alias across the back was very fitting, displaying her D-cups and the pinch of her waist. Her spandex shorts left almost nothing to the imagination. In her Retro Jordans, she tread toward the bar to grab a tray to begin her shift. When she'd started her job, she couldn't believe the amount of people that came into the place in the afternoon. Yet, one taste of the cook's hot wings, she could understand. That and the fact that the owner would put a few popular girls on the stage between the hours of 11 A.M. and 4 P.M., just to keep the place jumping like it was.

Flex entered with his sister, searching the area for his grandfather. He didn't want to be there, just being out of prison for a day. He wanted to remain in his home and eat all he wanted, when he wanted. Once he spotted the older man in the VIP section with a hookah up to his lips, he smirked and pulled Sincere by the hand.

Felix stood when he noticed his grandchildren coming toward him, and straightened his gray and black dress shirt. To see his grandson again was like heaven. Though he was still angry at him for taking a sentence to get the law off his back, he could still arrive into town just to spend time with him.

Felix spread his arms with a smile on his pale colored face. "My son."

"Padrè," Flex greeted him with a smile. "How are you?"

"I should be asking you." He surveyed his grandson closely, noticing that he had let his hair grow only so much that he could see his natural curls. He could tell that his grandson's visit to the barber the day before was an adventurous one. His grandson had dyed a quarter of his goatee silver, leaving it in a beautiful streak. "Trying to get much older on me, I see," he joked.

"Not really. Can we talk?"

"About me be angry with you? No. Today, I just want to enjoy the children I raised. No business talk until tomorrow. I'm worn out, Caesar. Traveling from country to country to remain under the radar is almost killing me. Your old man is not as vigorous as he used to be. But since I'm also one hell of a marksman, I'd say that I have no choice but to continue to travel. We have the know how—"

"And they have the money." Flex bumped fists with his grandfather before hiking up the legs of his jeans to take a seat on the curved sofa.

Sincere sat across from her brother and crossed her thick legs that extended from a pair of skin-tight shorts.

"Sin," Felix called his granddaughter as he leaned against the back of the couch. He was ready to tell her about her outfit of choice for the day.

"Old Dad?" she asked smartly.

"Welcome to Lush Cabaret," a sweet voice greeted them, cutting the tension.

Flex looked over, yet his words were stuck in his throat.

"Is there anything I can get you all? Appetizers to start? A private dance from our variety of talented girls?"

"Yes," Sincere spoke up. "Can we have a forty-piece hot wing. Half barbecue, please. I'd also like a mimosa and a Sprite."

Felix cleared his throat. "I'd like a Paul Masson on the rocks, the sliders, and can I get hot sauce on the side?"

The young woman nodded as she jotted their orders on her notepad. When she looked over at Flex, her breath was stolen. Quickly, she recovered and widened her smile. "For you?"

He blinked and swallowed. "Yeah, uhh… Let me get a Jack Daniel's, dry. Y'all got curly fries?"

"We do." She giggled. "Would that complete your orders?"

"That's it," Sincere answered politely. "You can tell that me and my daddy come here all too much for us not to have to even pick up the menus." She grabbed the stack of leather-bound booklets and handed them over to the waitress.

"I'll be right back with your orders."

Flex watched her walk away and noticed that the only thing that had changed about the young woman was that she had gained a little weight, but it fit her. Her figure made his mouth water.

Sincere cleared her throat to grab her brother's attention.

He held up his finger and stood.

"Where are you going?"

"I'll be back." Flex took his leave with his sights pasted on the waitress. He maneuvered through the busy visitors until he was near the bar, where she was putting in their orders for their drinks. "Sasha," he called her.

She looked over, finding that Flex was approaching her. She threw her last ticket over the bar and fast-paced toward the ramp that led to the locker room. She knew that the bodyguard wouldn't let him back there, no matter who he was.

"Sasha, wait!" he called for her, damn near on her heels.

The guard stretched his arm out, touching the wall after Sasha passed. "My bad, Flex," he said sympathetically. "I can't let you go back there. Welcome home, by the way."

"Then go and get her, Burner," he replied desperately.

"I can't do that either."

"Fuck!" He spun around and turned right back around to the man who was almost five inches taller, who also weighed about a hundred more pounds than he did. "You tell Sasha, whenever she comes out of that locker room, that this ain't over. She can't just act like she don't know me. I'll be seeing her lil' ass."

"Yo, Flex, calm down before you cause a scene," Burner reasoned. "Listen, her shift is over at eight, alright? Be here. I always escort the girls to the parking lot out back after every shift."

"Good lookin'."

"Ain't a thang. Keep ya head up. Glad to see you back home."

Flex eyed him closely. "What does that mean?"

"It means that you need to check ya' boy Charlie. Dude come in here almost every other night, leavin' with chicks like Sasha don't work here."

"Fuck does Charlie Boy have to do with Sasha?"

"You don't know?"

"Know what?"

"Shit, I'll let y'all talk it out."

Though Flex nodded, he had something else to add on to the fact that his own best friend hadn't reached out to him within the twenty-four hours that he had been out. Not only that, but he'd noticed how Charlie rarely sent him any mail.

He went back to the booth and sat right next to his sister, placing his Nike Air Max on the table in front of him.

"What's wrong?" she asked him.

"Explain to me why you failed to mention that Charlie is out here like he can't be marked?"

Sincere dropped her head. "Well, I didn't want to stress you out, brother. Charlie Boy hasn't been right since you've been in—"

"What the fuck does he have to do with Sasha?"

"Who?"

"Alley Cat. The girl who was just at the table."

"That was her? Damn, she looks different." She only knew the name *Alley Cat* because she'd heard her brother speak of the girl in a lover's tone. Only twice she'd seen the girl but from a distance.

"And you purposely chose to keep his bullshit away from me?"

"*Me*? What about you? What was that? What'd you chase Alley Cat down for?"

"That's nowhere near as important as you telling me why the hell you were keeping things away from me for, Sincere. Don't fuck with me."

She took a deep breath. "Charlie Boy was acting out. When I found out, I banned him from the operation until he could get himself together. I wasn't going to reward bad behavior."

"Was that so hard? Shows how well you know me. I would've appreciated your judgement. The only reason he was being a fool was because I wasn't with him."

"You shouldn't have to hold a grown man's hand, Caesar."

Felix spoke up as he grabbed the hookah from the middle of the table. "As much as I enjoy watching my children work and banter, this is not the time nor the place. Remember this. Now, after we get drinks and food, I want to see one of the new girls. Handle all of the drama later. Is that understood?"

"Yes, Padrè," they miserably answered in unison.

The family tried their best to enjoy the rest of their night, whereas Sasha refused to leave the locker room until someone told her that Flex had gone. She went into the restroom and cleaned her tear-stained cheeks, trying to swallow the hurt she was feeling over simply seeing him again.

The last time she had even spoken to him was right before she had gotten with Charlie. For weeks, Charlie had been relentless when trying to capture her attention, but she was too wrapped up in someone she thought really saw her for who she was. A young king by the name of Caesar Romina, who went by the street name "Flex". They flirted occasionally and talked over the phone periodically. He convinced her that the line of work he was in was too dangerous for them to go public. Yet, it seemed as though the rumors about Flex were true, when she overheard a gossiping group of girls in the nail salon, on the night of her junior prom, cackling about a Spanish beauty who he had been seen with.

Flex showed up to prom with the curvaceous girl on his arm, to which Sasha swallowed hard and left. She never accepted his calls, never returned his emails or texts, and the only one who seemed to be there for her was Charlie. She fell into his charisma and charm and didn't look back. It wasn't until she revealed that she was pregnant when the abuse started. Often times, she felt as if her son was the way he was because of Charlie's mighty hand, but that couldn't have been the case.

Sasha dried her cheeks and pulled her phone from her bra to check the time. She saw then that her sister had sent her yet another text, complaining about her very own nephew. It was the routine that she had whenever she looked after him. Sasha was over it and couldn't wait until her mother returned from her three-week vacation so she could look after Dean.

After changing her attire, she clicked on her Lyft app on her phone to hail a car. She already knew that Charlie wasn't going to be outside waiting for her. Just as Burner opened the door for the girls to leave, Sasha stepped through but was met with a bouquet of white roses.

Some of the girls sucked their teeth and went about their business, yet Sasha stood there and kept her eyes on the roses. Burner purposely hurried and closed the door so that Sasha couldn't come back in.

Dressed in a black and gray Nike Tech suit with a pair of polished rectangular specs was Flex. His thick bottom lip was caged between his teeth. He was nervously awaiting her to take his gift.

She rolled her eyes and walked past him to stand on the curb and wait for her Lyft.

"Come on, Sasha. I hadn't seen you in ages," he begged.

"Really?" She scoffed. "It didn't kill you, I see."

"I went to prison."

"Oh, I see," she said dryly. "I see that didn't kill you either. I was kind of hoping that you would get some kind of STD from that fake Jessica Rabbit you showed up to prom with."

Flex squinted. "Is this why you're mad at me? Sasha. That girl was an escort. She was paid to be with me for my eighteenth birthday and to accompany me to prom. That's it."

"You could've told me that, Caesar."

"I was trying, but you never returned my calls. I never meant to hurt you."

"So what was all that talk about you being with some girl? It wasn't me."

Flex could see the pain in her eyes and hear it in her voice. "Please, just let me make it up to you."

"So much time has passed, Caesar." She bowed her head and shook it. "I don't believe you can make up for it all."

A car pulled up in front of her that had a purple light on the dashboard.

Sasha moved past him and got inside, concealing the

tears that she was holding. There was so much she wanted to say and ask, but she decided against it.

Flex was left standing there with his bouquet as the car rode away. He had too many words roaming through his mind and didn't have enough time to get them all out.

CHAPTER THREE

Eight Years Prior

Flex placed his finger up to his lips as he led Sasha up the stairs of his grandfather's home. She clutched her lip with her teeth while tiptoeing up the marble staircase. Sasha knew that they could easily get into trouble for sneaking, but it was exciting to her. Flex wrapped his arms around her waist when they reached the top of the steps, and hungrily kissed her lips. She dropped her head, placing her hand over her mouth so she wouldn't laugh aloud.

He nodded in the direction of the hall where they used soft feet to head toward his bedroom. Once inside, he kissed her more passionately, tightening his grip around her waist, with one hand sliding down to her ample backside.

Sasha closed the door, leaning her head back. "Don't act like you want me that badly, Flex," she whispered.

"I told you to call me Caesar," he grumbled. "And if I didn't want you, I wouldn't have sneaked you into the house."

Being a year younger than him, Sasha thought she struck gold with young Flex. Her life was dull and boring until he picked her out of a crowd at a pool party, just to have fun with her and her only. Since he had his own cabana and Jacuzzi, no one ever knew that she was there. No one but him and Charlie.

Flex's phone vibrated inside his back pocket, just as he leaned in for another kiss. He smacked his lips and backed away so he could answer the call.

Sasha folded her arms and leaned against the door. To her, work was always calling, interrupting their alone time, but she never voiced it.

When Flex hung up the phone, he turned to her with apologetic eyes.

"Just take me home," she mumbled.

"Sasha, I'm sorry. My Old Dad needs me. I can make it up to you, I promise."

"You always do," she said with a half-smile.

Flex met her lips again, this time gently sucking on them. It made her lightly squirm against his hard body.

Present Day

"Sasha! Sasha, get the fuck up!" Charlie screamed.

Her eyes fluttered open to see that her boyfriend was standing over her with a grimace on his surly face. She knew she couldn't have done anything wrong. He couldn't have known about Flex speaking to her days prior. She'd even gone as far as to call out of work but use her son as an excuse to do so.

"Why the fuck is you moaning in your sleep?"

She chose not to respond. Instead, she rolled over and closed her eyes again.

"You must be dreamin' about one of them niggas from your job," he complained. "If I find out you fuckin' any one of 'em—"

"You wouldn't find out because I'm not doing anything," she said below a whisper.

"What?" he hissed. "What you say to me?"

She rolled over and sat up to look him in the eyes. "I said that I'm not doing anything, Charlie. You don't have to constantly assume anything negative about me when I'm innocent. I've been nothing but devoted to you, yet I find empty condom wrappers in your pants all the—"

"Fuck you doin' goin' through my pants for?"

"That's not the point I'm trying to make."

"You gon' learn to mind your fuckin' business." Charlie snatched the covers off of her, grabbed her leg with one hand, and unbuckled his belt with the other.

Successfully, she kicked him off and jumped off the bed.

She was headed for the master's bath when he caught her by the back of the neck and slung her to the floor. The next thing Sasha could feel through the jersey she wore to bed was the stinging pain of his leather belt. She screamed and kicked at him until she found the strength to crawl her way up to the bathroom door, where she crossed the threshold, attempting to close the door with her foot.

With all his strength, Charlie barged in and threw the belt into the shower. "So, you're running away from me?

You fuckin' other niggas, goin' through my shit, and you're runnin' away from me instead of talkin' this out?"

"I'm not fucking anybody!" she screamed, with tears rolling down her cheeks.

Charlie slapped her across the face and let his pants fall. "Yeah, we gon' see."

"No, Charlie!" She cried, with her hands stretched out in front of her.

After he freed his manhood from his boxers, he violently pulled at her panties until he had enough access to her center. Mercilessly, he forced himself inside of her, breathing heavily into the crook of her neck. "You're wet as fuck, and you mean to tell me that you hadn't been fuckin' nobody else?"

She couldn't respond while trying to keep her screams and pleas at bay. She didn't want to wake Dean or expose him to the things that his father had been doing to her.

When he was finished, he pulled his rod out, splashing his semen onto her thigh. "You need to clean yourself up, hoe. You want to know why I got those condom wrappers in my pocket? It's 'cause I don't want no more kids.

Especially not none like the motherfucker who you can't keep goddamn quiet when I'm trying to sleep." He tapped her on the forehead, then rose to his feet in the bathroom. "I'll tell you why I need outside pussy. It's 'cause yours ain't been the same since you spat out that fuckin' crybaby you got. You need to handle your business more seriously before you and him be out on the curb, in the cold. And tell Monique to stop fuckin' textin' me about that boy when she's keepin' him. I got a real job, where I need to fuckin' focus. That lil' chump change you make at that cabaret ain't shit. Tighten the fuck up, Sasha. I'm tired of playin' games with you."

She lay there on the floor shivering until she heard the bathroom door in the hall close. Slowly but surely, she was piecing together an exit strategy. Dean was getting too old, and she was getting too tired of the bullshit that came with Charlie.

The next morning was no different. When Sasha rose from the bed and headed into the kitchen, she was met by digits around her neck. Charlie was a half an inch away

32

from her face when he spat, "I'm done playin' fuckin' games with you, Sasha."

She clawed at his wrist to get him to loosen his grip. "What are you talking about?"

"Either you stop workin' at that joint or you're out of here. I see the shit you got to wear. I ain't havin' my woman walk around in booty shorts in front of other niggas."

"Let me go. I can't breathe."

He shoved her into the wall before releasing her. "I don't want to deal with none of this shit. Until you can get yourself together, you're on your own."

"What are you talking about?"

Charlie walked toward the door of their small home when he stopped and turned around. "You think this is the life I wanted? You think I wanted to live with a hoe-ass, weak-ass bitch and some retar—"

"Don't you dare!"

"Who the fuck are you screaming at?" Charlie charged toward her and threw a fist at her face so hard that it split her eyebrow.

When Sasha fell to the floor, he took his foot to her ribs repeatedly. Dean screaming in the background didn't even make him stop.

CHAPTER FOUR

In a daze, Sasha could hear Charlie in the bedroom, on his phone. She gulped and pushed herself off the carpet. Any decision she made prior to this moment was nothing compared to what she knew she was capable of doing. She looked down and found that Dean was laying right next to her, facing her silently. She pressed her finger up to her lips and rose with a sore body. Gently she grabbed his hand to bring him up to his feet. Quietly, she walked to the front door with fear in her heart that Charlie would chase after her. The only thought that pushed it to the back of her mind was that he had left her there on that carpet so long that the blood from her brow was dry and cracked.

Bravely, she placed her hand on the knob and twisted so fast that it was a blur. She swung her son in front of her and squeezed him tight as she prayed for God to give her speed and strength. The higher power responded by allowing Sasha to run away from that horrid place in nothing but an undershirt, panties, and her pajama-clad son whose limbs were wrapped tightly around her torso and neck.

She didn't care who was looking at her and why. She didn't care where she was going, just as long as it was away from Charlie.

A silver-colored Ford cut her off before she could clear another block. Out of it jumped a guy she once knew from school. He placed his hands in the air as he approached her. "It's cool, Alley Cat," he said in a calm voice. "I saw you runnin' with your lil' one. Flex told seven of us to keep a close watch on you because you seemed jumpy. He wanted answers."

Sasha let out a breath she didn't realize she was holding in as tears poured down her cheeks.

"Come on. Get in. I'll take you wherever you tryna go."

She reluctantly obliged, still holding on tightly to Dean. Sasha hadn't even noticed that she didn't tell Black, the guy who seemed to save her some travel time, where to take her until he pulled into a gate. "Where are we?"

He looked into the rearview mirror and gave her a smile, showcasing all of his silver teeth. "You never spoke up, so I guess this is where you need to be."

As he pulled along the circular head of the drive, Sasha's heart could've fallen out of her chest when she noticed Flex standing on the porch of his large, two-story home.

Hurriedly, he pulled open the backdoor, and all Sasha could see of him were the 360 waves of his hair and the tattoo on his arm when he reached for Dean. Then, he extended his hand to her for her to take it and get out.

"You could've told me that you had a kid, Sasha," he said as his fingers slipped inside of hers.

Sasha's head popped up at Dean's head laying comfortably against Flex's chest. "You must have a very kind heart, because Dean doesn't like strangers."

"Yeah, well, I shouldn't be a stranger to him anyway."

Flex showed Sasha where she could clean her face then gave her a pair of his shorts so that he could get her to a hospital to have a proper evaluation. Though she opposed, he promised her that he wouldn't be going anywhere. He'd remain at her side.

While waiting for the doctor and all the x-ray results, the two caught up and told each other what they had been going through. She revealed that she could've sworn that she was in love with Charlie after her heartbreak and after Flex seemed to just vanish. He, in turn, disclosed the fact that he never wanted anyone. All he wanted was the fast money. But a charmer with a sense of humor and understanding forced him to fall in love. Only, he couldn't tell her because he had already broken her heart.

When the results were revealed, Sasha was only lucky that Charlie's feet weren't as mighty as his hand, because her ribs were only bruised. She was advised to take it easy for the next three to six weeks. She promised that she would but made sure that Flex didn't get the wrong idea. She had him to take her and Dean to her mother's home, where she knew she would be welcomed. She'd sacrifice listening to her mother cuss and fuss over what had happened to her daughter. Sasha just wanted her son in a safe place now.

Flex, on the low, had four of his goons to go into

Charlie's home and take out all of Sasha and Dean's belongings, having them to throw it all in trash bags.

Over the course of a month, Flex didn't take any chances. He had someone to look after Sasha's mother's house around the clock, just to make sure that Charlie wouldn't get the wrong idea after he was fired from the operation and go to look for Sasha to mooch off her. During that time, he sent a fresh floral arrangement every other week along with an edible arrangement. When going to work, Sasha had to be driven there by someone who worked for Flex. He didn't want to suffocate her, but he wanted her to know and feel that she was safe.

It took him a month to weigh her down and ask her out on their first official date, and it took her that long just to say yes. She needed a break from Charlie clowning around on Facebook like his life was just perfect after getting rid of her and their son. Flex made up for that too. Not only did he treat Sasha to her first five-star dinner, but he wanted to do something that Dean might've liked too.

Surprisingly, he took to Flex and often pointed to cars

on TV or in magazines that reminded him of Flex's car. Flex made it a point to learn the boy, like his triggers, his dislikes and likes, his needs, his wants, how to read him and all. The first time Flex and Dean spent time together, Dean threw a fit which caught Flex off guard, but he handled himself in a manner that Sasha didn't think was possible. Instead of telling her to shut him up, Flex kneeled and spoke in a soft voice to get him to calm down, then encouraged him with toys or books to take his mind off of whatever it was that triggered him in the first place. That in itself sealed the deal. Sasha had to admit to herself that. when all was said and done, she had experienced what was now the best four whole months of her life. She had even moved out of her mother's and had gotten her own place. Thanks to Flex bribing management and security, they made sure to keep Charlie away from Sasha's job so she could work in peace and keep her sense of independence.

Within the last two weeks, Charlie had been on hands and knees in her messages, even going as far as presenting an anger management certificate. He begged her to at least let him spend time with Dean to prove to her that he was sorry and that he could be a better man. Against her better judgement, she told him that he had one shot. She also told him that he'd better not fuck it up because there was someone who wouldn't mind taking him out.

As she peered in the mirror at her smooth, chocolate complexion, she smiled. She hadn't received a bruise, a scar, or a welt. Sasha was finally happy and in a good headspace. However, the moment that she had to drop off Dean at the old house, Flex clenched his jaw. He didn't have a good feeling about any of what was going on. He waited in the car, as requested, for Sasha to return. By no means did he want to mess up the surprise he had in store for her.

He slapped on a smile for the ride to the restaurant and even through their meals. Once the dessert was placed on the table, Sasha could've lost her mind. Laying atop her New York style cheesecake was a canary yellow diamond ring surrounded by solitaires.

"Sasha, I've never met anyone like you before, and you know I was wild as hell," Flex told her. "As clearly as I can see that I make you and Dean happy, I just want you to know that you do that for me too. Just please tell me that you'll let us continue to do this for the rest of our lives."

"Yes!" she screamed, leaping out of her seat to lace her arms around his neck. This had been the first time Sasha cried in a long while, but this time, they were happy tears.

She couldn't stop staring at her ring or keep her tears at bay during dessert. She truly was happy.

CHAPTER FIVE

Charlie thought that his smile and his soft voice would last forever with Dean. He could've sworn that if he proved himself to his son, then he could easily lead Sasha into believing that he had changed, and it would, in turn, make her come back home.

Dean sat at the dinner table with his head bowed. For the first time, Charlie had noticed the part in his son's fresh haircut. He wondered how Sasha was able to get him to sit still. Out of all the five years thus far, after Dean's first birthday, he had been too embarrassed to take his son to the barber. On his first birthday, Dean threw a fit when the barber had come too close with the clippers in his hand. Charlie didn't understand his own son and had become furious with the tantrum. *It must be her new dude*, he thought.

Charlie nudged the plate closer to his six-year-old, hoping he'd eat his three green bean stalks that were lined next to each other but weren't touching, and his mound of mashed potatoes. "You got to eat," he said lowly with mercy in his eyes. "Dean, come on, man. You ain't ate nothin' since your mama left. I know you miss her. I miss her too, but she ain't comin' back unless you ea—"

Suddenly, Dean flipped the plate over, splashing his potatoes in Charlie's face. Dean's eyes stayed focused on the rolling green beans until they had fallen off the table.

Slowly, Charlie slid his wide hand down his face. He saw red. How could he have possibly gathered the thought that this child— his *ex's* child— would want to cooperate?

He lost it. All of his patience and the act of being kind to the difficult boy had gone out of the window and around the corner. He stood, simultaneously raising Dean out of his seat by the collar of his designer shirt. All the way to the front door, he dragged his frail son and opened it. Afterward, he shook him, screaming in his face, "You ungrateful motherfucker! You never liked me anyway! I don't need you! You stupid fucker! You're the reason your mama ain't here! She don't love your ass!"

Dean spat in Charlie's face while trying to claw the

man's hands away from his collar.

Charlie used all of his strength to throw the boy across the hall, slamming his back against the wall. Charlie obviously miscalculated how far away the wall was from the stairs. As soon as Dean landed onto the ground and rolled, trying to catch his footing, he tumbled down the steel and concrete steps, with his thumps and bumps chorusing until he landed at the bottom.

Charlie's chest rose and fell, even when looking over the banister at the damage he had done. Dean lay on the concrete with his arms spread, his legs in a figure four, and his eyes closed. It would've been easy for Charlie to simply go downstairs and retrieve him, had it not been for the crimson forming a perfect halo as it had grown in width around Dean's head.

Frightful, Charlie stepped back into the apartment with his hand clasped over his mouth. His eyes were wide once he snapped out of his angry trance. On a whim, he stepped back out, screaming, "Help me! My son fell down the stairs! Somebody call for help! Please, somebody help!"

With only his own voice echoing back to him, he

rushed down the steps, pulling his cellphone from his back pocket.

Sasha pulled her lips away from Flex's, with her cheeks burning from all the blushing, laughing, and talking she had been doing all afternoon. After dinner, Flex took her for a walk in the park. With her neck leaned back, she was lost inside his odd colored eyes.

"What're you thinking about?" he grumbled as he tightened his arms around her waist.

"You."

"I'm standing right here, though. What're you thinking about me for, Sasha?"

"Just wondering if I should say this now or later."

"Say what? You plottin' on me?"

"No." She giggled. "I was going to say... I'm—" Her ringing cellphone interrupted her. Since it was Charlie's ringtone, she hurried to answer, thinking that it was about Dean. "Yeah?"

"Baby," he cried. "They're takin' Dean to the ER! It ain't good!"

"What?" she shrieked, whirling away from Flex. "What are you talking about? What happened to him?"

"Babe?" Flex whispered as he stepped in front of her to gently grab her elbows. "What's wrong?"

"He was playing in the hall and fell down the stairs!" Charlie lied hysterically.

Sasha hung up her phone. She tried to maintain her tears, but there was no use in fighting them. She should've known to follow her first mind along with Flex's paranoia.

"What, S? Talk to me, baby."

"We need to go to the hospital," she said with a sniffle. "Dean fell down the stairs."

"What?"

She left him standing in front of the restaurant as she headed to the car with haste in her stride.

Flex's brows pressed as he reached for his phone in the front pocket of his jeans. After clicking on a contact, he pressed his phone to his ear. "Sin. I need you to meet me somewhere in about forty-five minutes. This shit ain't about to be cute at all. My lil' dude supposedly fell down some stairs, but I smell bullshit. Texting you the address."

He hung up and jogged to the car, knowing that Dean was too careful to fall down a set of stairs. The little one didn't even play on the stairs he had in Flex's home, let alone having a desire to do it in public.

Sasha barreled out of the elevator first, searching the signs on the walls for room numbers. The informer on the first floor let her know exactly where she could find Dean, and she wasn't worried about anything else at the moment. Not even the fact that her erratic breathing was giving her a headache.

"Baby." Charlie sighed as he stood from a chair in the hall. He spread his arms for his ex, only to be dodged.

Through a small window, she could see her son laying on the bed with his head wrapped in gauze. It broke her heart, but it angered her more. Given the fact that he wasn't dead, it gave her leeway to turn to Charlie and muster up some courage that she never had. Sasha reached back to sophomore year of high school and slapped the grill out of Charlie's mouth.

The force caused him to spin and hit his head against

the wall behind him. When he caught himself, he turned, expecting to return the blow. What he was faced with was a brown-skinned guy who was a little taller than him. "What the fuck are you doing here?" he lashed.

Flex decided not to return a statement. He turned to Sasha, turned her around, and made her focus through the window so they could watch while Dean was being cared for. Slowly, he rocked from side to side with her, trying to get her to calm down.

"I should've listened," she whimpered. "You told me, and I didn't listen. Baby, I didn't even listen to myself."

"Don't do that." Flex cooed her. "It's alright. Thankfully, he's alive."

"What if—"

"We're not doing that, Sasha. He's alive. We're just going to keep a more watchful eye. That's all."

Suddenly, all three adults heard a familiar scream. It made Sasha crack even more.

"It's alright, babe. I got it, alright?"

"Hell, naw!" Charlie yelled. "*I'm* his father! I got it. Where the fuck you even come from, Flex? You fuckin' my wife? We were boys, and I didn't even know that you were out of prison, dawg!"

Accompanied by Flex's glare, Sasha whirled around to him with a grimace that Charlie had never seen before.

"You've done enough," she harshly said to him.

Flex had already opened the door and held his hand up to the nurse who was a little too close to Dean. His bonus son didn't like strange people, and he knew so. "Give me a minute, alright," he politely told the nurse. He inched closer to the bed and sat on the edge. To him, it was obvious that Dean was shaken up. He refused to look Flex in the eyes. "What's up, buddy?" he lowly greeted Dean. "You want to tell me what happened?"

Dean scratched at his IV that was placed on top of his hand with his eyes never resting.

Sasha's hand reached her son's before Flex's could.

Dean almost leaped out of the bed to hug his mother. She returned his squeeze with a fresh set of tears rolling down her cheeks.

Flex gave a simple nod to insert whatever it was the nurse was about to give Dean inside of his IV while he was distracted.

"Ms. Marshall?" someone asked from the doorway.

The couple looked back to see two policemen in uniform.

"May we have a word?"

Sasha looked between Dean and Flex then at the officer who was speaking. "Sure. Sure. What's this about?"

"We need a moment in private, ma'am."

"Babe, just go," Flex urged her. "I'm here."

She lightly nodded then kissed her son's bandaged forehead.

Dean lay back on his pillows, feeling the effects of his morphine running through his veins. Flex took his eyes over to a distressed Charlie in the hall. With a snarl, he rose from the bed and exited the room, gently closing the door behind him.

Charlie got out of his seat and stuck his chest out to Flex as if it would scare him anyway.

"Let me find out that he was pushed, thrown, tossed, or so much as nudged down those steps, and that's an open throat for you, patna," Flex promised. "I don't give a fuck if he had so much as been *told* to go and play by those damn stairs."

"Who you think you talkin' to? You forgettin' who I am, Flex? Huh?"

"I'm talkin' to a lame ass fuck boy that I expect to be guilty. Your kind is *weak*," he hissed with a quivering lip. "It's the only reason niggas like you put your hands on females and pick on kids. You're a coward, and I expect to get rid of you. You are poison to my family, kid." Mockingly, he tapped Charlie on the cheek before he left.

Passing the visitor's room, Flex politely knocked on the pane of the door and invited himself in. He kissed Sasha's forehead.

"Where are you going?" she asked with worry in her voice.

"I'll be right back, babe. Dean is resting. I need to catch up with my old man right quick."

She tugged at his large hand. "Please... come back."

"You never have to worry about something like that. Of course I'm coming back."

Sasha lightly nodded as she let his hand slip from hers.

As expected, Sin had gotten out of her black Mercedes, ready to see what could've possibly happened to her nephew. Even she was in love with Dean and learned about him just in case she had to babysit or if there was a chance that she would somehow be alone with the special needs child.

Flex gave his sister a hug then led her in the direction of Sasha's old apartment.

"What are we looking for?" Sin asked her brother as she followed.

"Dude say my boy fell down the stairs."

"And it's bullshit."

"Exactly. The thing about Dean is that he's too specific. There could be a possibility that this dude is telling the truth if Dean was sporadic, but he's not." Flex stopped at the bottom of the stairs when he saw the pool of dried blood that painted the concrete. He gulped the rage that was rising to the top and stepped over it. Taking backward steps, he canvassed each stair with his eyes until he reached the top, then took his focus to the right of him.

"That's a pretty nice sized dent," Sin said, sliding on a pair of white gloves that she snagged from her glove compartment.

As a safety measure, Flex pulled his own set from his back pocket that he had gotten out of his armrest. He was clenching his jaw at the thought of Dean being pushed so hard that he dented the thin steel pleats of the wall.

The two stood by the door of the apartment while Sin used her skills to jimmy the lock to get the door open.

As soon as they stepped over the threshold, Sin spread her arms at the mess in the small dining area. "Jackpot." She chuckled.

With furrowed brows, Flex took hard, slow steps over to the messy table and overturned chair. Three single stalks of green beans lay on the floor with splatters of potatoes everywhere. "See what I mean, Sin? Dean is this specific. Broccoli, green beans, asparagus… it can only be three, they can't touch, and he has to dip them inside his mashed potatoes."

Sin squatted to see underneath the table and squinted. "Well, all three green beans are here, so your little one didn't eat a damn thing."

"Which caused this asshole to lose his temper." Flex pointed out of the open door at the wall across the hall. "He drags him out of the door, flings him across the hall, and… I'm not sure if he pushed him or kicked him down the steps. Those stairs are so close to that wall that I can't tell."

"Well, we know what happened to lead him against that wall, which is enough evidence in itself for you to give him an old-fashioned ass whoopin'. We know that Dean wasn't just playing near the goddamn stairs, so he lied. You should bust his head for that too."

Flex kept his eyes on the dent in the wall, trying his best to come to a conclusion as to how his bonus son had gone tumbling down the stairs. "I need to go back to the hospital."

"What for? To go round for round with him among witnesses?"

"No. We got a body to snatch."

CHAPTER SIX

Flex was on a ticking clock. He patiently waited for Charlie to finish giving his statement to the police and children's services before he asked for a word. Foolishly, Charlie rode the elevator down to the first floor and went into the darkened parking lot with someone who he used to consider a friend. Before they even reached Flex's car, a black bag was thrown over his head, and a black van pulled up behind them. The men struggled to get Charlie inside while Flex kept his pace to his car.

Not long after, they wound up at a place that Charlie was all too familiar with. His bag was snatched off, and he was bound by chains around his wrist, suspended from the concrete. When Flex stepped into the light, he instantly noticed how Flex checked his wrist watch.

"I'm going to ask you questions," Flex told him, "and I need you to answer them accordingly. No extra shit."

Sin appeared at her brother's side with a black rod in

56

her hand that had sparks flying out of the end of it. Another tall and bulky man stepped up next to her with his hands covered in white tape.

"You don't answer these questions appropriately and who knows what's going to happen to you."

"What the fuck, Flex?" Charlie whined. "You my boy. If you want Sasha, take her and leave me the fuck alone."

"See, that's where you fucked up, my dude. What about Dean?"

"You can have him too."

"Oh, how easy it is for you to turn over your entire family all because I have you in a compromising position. Where was all that at when you were at the hospital? Your chest was swollen then."

"Look, all this over a female ain't worth it."

"My *fiancée*, motherfucker."

Charlie looked up and could've sworn he heard Flex wrong.

"So, what's Dean's least favorite color?"

Charlie squinted.

"Oh, I know that!" Sin exclaimed, raising her free hand

in the air. "Tag me! Tag me! I know!"

"Blue," Charlie boldly answered on his own.

Sin shook her head. She forced the rod into Charlie's side, sending jolts of electricity through his body, ignoring his hollering.

Flex said, "It's red. What's Sasha's favorite song?"

"I don't know!" Charlie screamed.

"You don't know shit about your family, huh? But you can put hands on folks?"

The big man next to Sin stepped in front of Charlie and cracked his knuckles.

"What was it like for you, Charles? Hm? When you swung and heard a bone break?"

The fighter gave Charlie's ribs a mean right hook that rocked him and rattled the chains.

"Did it make you feel like a fuckin' man to hear her cry? Huh?" He talked over the smacks of skin and Charlie crying in agony. "Did it make you happy when you drew blood from her? You must've been hard when you choked the shit out of her and took away her self-esteem. Yeah, bitch nigga. And were you proud of yourself when my son went flying down the stairs and almost lost his life because of you?"

"Stop, man." Charlie cried with blood dripping out of his mouth.

"Stop? Stop what? Nah, it ain't no stop. Now, what you're going to do is sign over your parental rights to Dean. You give me trouble or so much as stall, I will kill you where you stand. Y'all, let him down and get his ass to the ER. Take him somewhere else. I don't want him near my family." Flex walked out of the warehouse, still angry at what had happened, but he had to get back to Sasha and Dean before she started to ask questions.

———————

Sasha sat on the side of her son's bed, watching as he slept. All that flooded her thoughts was that she could've lost him and that she was so stupid for trusting Charlie in the first place. Then, she thought of Flex. It wasn't unusual for him to tell her that he had something to do, but in the last few months, work didn't get in the way of anything when he was with her and Dean. She dropped her head, knowing that since Charlie was MIA and so was Flex that only the worst happened.

A tender hand touched her back as the sound of a chair softly scraping across the floor filled her ears. "They say anything while I was gone?" Flex asked her.

"No," she answered in a hoarse voice. "They'd given him stitches. I just thank God that he didn't crack his skull."

"Me too."

"What did you do to Charlie, Flex?"

He took in a breath, ready to tell her a lie. Upon grabbing her hand and taking a look at the rock he'd placed there, a lie was out of the question. "I had someone else to give him a beating that wouldn't amount to the ones he had given you. Then, I had them to take him to get looked at. He has an understanding that he's signing over his parental rights for Dean. I know you may be mad, but please understand that a real man doesn't put his hands on his woman, and he damn sure doesn't hurt an innocent child. Real love doesn't hurt. It doesn't leave a bruise, a scar, and it doesn't draw blood. Sasha, the only time I want you sore in the morning or can't stop crying is because I made love to you like neither of us have ever gone at it before. What I did to Charlie was give him his own medicine and the freedom he acted like he wanted."

"Flex, I have to tell you something important."

He kissed her hand and sat back in his seat, afraid that she was one step away from taking off her engagement ring because of his confession.

"We're having a baby," she said in a hushed tone. "I'm only four weeks along."

Flex hurriedly grabbed her face and kissed her lips.

"Everything is right on time. Us, the move, the engagement—"

"Like it's supposed to be," he whispered. "Our son will heal, but how do we tell him that he's going to be a big brother?"

"I don't know." She quietly chuckled.

"How about we just relax for now, huh? We can take wedding planning and telling Dean about the baby as slowly as possible."

Sasha rested her head on Flex's shoulder, with her eyes on her son in the hospital bed. Even though she faced tragedy, she was still fortunate, and with a quickness, Flex made her a happy woman again. It was by Charlie's mighty hand that broke her and forced her to find herself. That same hand pushed her right into the arms of someone who actually loved her and her son unconditionally and who wouldn't hurt them. Sasha smiled at the thought. Finally, there was no pain, no misery, no questioning herself, or having to be overprotective of her son, afraid that he might be hurt. It was only… happiness and peace.

He Loved Me to Death

By Sparkle Lewis

Synopsis

Quaysha Merritt had everything going for herself. She was beautiful, intelligent, and the daughter of a well-respected pastor. Though her parents were strict, Quaysha did everything in her power to abide by their rules, until Shawn Rivers came along.

Shawn Rivers was the star quarterback of the local high school's football team and known on the streets as a ladies' man. As charming as he was, Shawn had a dark side to him. When he first started dating the beautiful Quaysha Merritt, to say he was smitten with her would be an understatement. In fact, he was so in love with her that he proposed to her while they were still in high school.

After being kicked out of the house by her parents, Quaysha was left no choice but to move in with Shawn. All of a sudden, things began to change. The once charming boy that could do no wrong in her eyes and had been her saving grace on many occasions had become a threat to her existence. She endured years of verbal, emotional, sexual, and physical abuse at the hands of the man that vowed to love her.

Can Quaysha escape Shawn's clutches before it's too late, or will her escape cost her, her life?

Acknowledgments and Dedication

Thank you for every reader, family member, friend, and author in the industry that supports me. My pen would stop working without you.

For everyone that has gone through or is going through any type of domestic violence situation, please, I beg you, seek help. As a two-time survivor, I cannot stress it enough that I refused to go through it a third time, knowing I may not be so lucky. I cannot stress it enough that *you* don't have to go through it. Please... seek the help you need. Put an end to it now before the choice is no longer yours. This one is for you...

Loving you was good...

Quaysha

"Baeee, I gotta go," I told Shawn while I tried to keep his hand from roaming up my leg. I was already out an hour later than my curfew, and I knew my parents were going to kill me.

"Come on, baby. Just let me get it one more time, pleeeease?" he begged, causing me to get wet all over again. But logic outweighed me wanting to please him or myself. My parents would put me on a punishment so harsh, I wouldn't be able to leave the house until I graduated high school, and that was two more years.

Shawn and I started dating when we were freshmen. At first, my father was against it because Shawn had somewhat of a reputation around town, but Shawn came to him like a man—even at fourteen—and eventually, my father gave in, allowing me to date him.

What we had was nothing short of amazing, and it was true what they said: opposites do attract. I was a preacher's kid, grew up in a loving two-parent household, an only child, and had everything handed to me on a silver platter. Well, everything that was in my parents' means. For some reason, everyone thought being a preacher's kid, I would rock the best clothes, shoes, and keep my hair in all the latest styles. Maybe that was true for the kids whose father was the pastor of a huge church, but my father's congregation consisted of twenty members, and fifteen of them were family.

Most of my clothes came from Goodwill, and my shoes either came from Shoe Show, which was a thousand seasons behind, or Payless. Needless to say, while other girls were rocking the newest J's, Quaysha was rocking Reeboks or wannabe J's with the man jumping in the opposite direction. Shawn, on the other hand, lived with his brother, wore the best gear money could buy, and his shoe game reached a level beyond any of the dudes at our school.

When he approached me, I thought it was a joke. I

mean, he could have any girl at the school that he wanted. Hell, even teachers were checking for him. So for him to want *me*, it blew me away. Shawn was six feet two, dark skinned, had short dreads, and the body of a buffed god. Shawn was literally *that* dude.

That was a year ago, and here we were, still holding strong, something honorable to be said, especially with the way dudes switched girls at my school.

"So can I just eat you out?" Shawn asked, and as tempted as I was, I still said no. He had just taken my virginity three weeks ago, and we'd been sexing like two horny ass teenagers—which we were—ever since.

"Damn... aight."

I could hear the frustration in his voice, and though I didn't want him to be mad at me, if I wanted our little sexcapades to continue, I knew it was best I hightailed my behind home.

Shawn pulled up at my house fifteen minutes later. By now, he was over his little pissy fit of not being able to

70

sample the goods one more time.

"You think you gon' be able to make it to my game Friday night?

"Of course, babe. I wouldn't miss it for the world. Unless these two are trippin', and then I'll have to make up for it another time," I replied to him, gently stroking his cheek.

Before I got out the car, I gave Shawn one last kiss and told him I'd see him in school tomorrow. Once he made sure I was in the house, he pulled off. Lord, how I wish I could have left with him because as soon as I turned around from closing the door, there stood both of my parents, grilling the hell out of me.

"Quaysha Monique Merritt, do you see what time it is?" my father started.

"Daddy, I am so sorry. Shawn's car stalled on the way home from the library, and we had to wait until his brother picked us up," I said, quickly reciting the line I'd rehearsed a million times in my head.

"Why didn't you pick up the phone and call someone?" my mother asked.

"I apologize, Mom. I didn't think it was going to take his brother half an hour to get to us, and when it finally dawned on me to call, my phone was dead," I replied, showing my mother my dead phone.

"I kept it on silent while we were at the library, just in case either of you called, but I didn't think to charge it while I was there. I'm sorry."

I knew telling them that I was thinking of them by keeping my phone on, which was against the library's rules, would help my case.

"Well what was wrong with the car?" my father asked, and jut like that, I knew I was off the hook.

"His brother hadn't gotten an oil change in forever, and it messed up the engine. He's going to have to let Shawn use one of his other cars now to get back and forth to school. Dreek can be so irresponsible sometimes," I said, shaking my head to add emphasis to my story.

I hated that it had to come to this—me lying to my parents just to sneak out and spend time with Shawn—but I knew they would never let us do anything more than study dates and me going to his games.

"OK, sweetie. Go to your room and get ready for school tomorrow."

"Yes, ma'am. I love you, guys," I responded, kissing both of my parents on the cheek.

When I got to my room, I plopped down on the bed and sighed. I had dodged another bullet, thank God. Well... I didn't know if thanking God was the right thing to do, considering the bullet I dodged was for reasons He wouldn't approve of. Nevertheless, I was in the clear once again, and for that, I was more than thankful.

***

Friday was here before I knew it, and I was beyond excited. I had convinced my parents to let me spend the night at my best friend, Keyonna's, house. What they were unaware of was the fact that Keyonna's parents were out of town tonight and wouldn't be back until tomorrow evening. I was going to stay with Shawn after the game and then go to Keyonna's tomorrow so her parents would automatically assume I had been there the entire weekend. Therefore, if my parents asked them in church Sunday, which they never missed a Sunday of going, then all they could say was what they saw.

What put the icing on the cake and made it even better was that Keyonna was messing around with Shawn's older brother, Dreek, so she would be with us tonight. Her parents did have a home phone, so they would be calling her cell phone. Voila. I would be with her. Case closed.

I woke up feeling refreshed. This would be the first time Shawn and I would actually spend the night with each other and also the first time we would have sex in a bed. Yes, I allowed him to take my virginity in the back of his Impala, and I didn't regret it. Sex in a car at the lake was so bomb for me.

"Quaysha, are you coming home from school or going

straight to Keyonna's house?" my mother asked when I walked into the kitchen. I really didn't feel like sitting down for breakfast—that's how amped up I was.

"I'm going to come by and get my clothes first, and then we're going to the game," I responded. They never had issues with me going to the game, so I didn't have a problem offering that information.

"OK, sweetie. Have a good day at school, and enjoy yourself at the game and this weekend."

"I will. And oh, shoot a prayer up for me. I have a test in Civics today. I know I'll ace it, but too much prayer never hurts," I said. She looked at me and smiled, which I knew she would considering I mentioned prayer. After I gave her a hug and kiss, I headed out the door to walk to the bus stop.

When I got further up the street, I could hear the system before I actually saw the car. I turned around as the music got closer and saw the car slowing down. Since I didn't recognize the car, I kept on about my business, but the car pulled up beside me. Once the driver's side window rolled down, I saw it was Shawn.

"Boy, whose car is this?" I asked, curious, because I had never seen this car. His brother had a fleet of cars, but this one in particular, I'd never seen.

"Dreek copped this yesterday. Come on," he said, and I walked around the car and jumped in.

"Why does Dreek need so many cars? Heck, what does he even do for a living?" I realized I didn't know much about his brother even though Shawn lived with him.

"He gets his bread by any means necessary. That's all you need to know," he replied, leaning over and kissing me on the cheek. Of course, I blushed. I always did whenever I was in his presence. If I wasn't blushing, I was getting butterflies. Shawn just had that effect on me.

We rode to school listening to "Drunk In Love" which described exactly how I was feeling. Though Shawn hated the song, he put it on repeat because I told him that we were the Jay and Bey of our town.

When we pulled up to the school, as usual, Shawn got

the flirtatious glances from the females, while I got the eye rolls, which didn't bother me at all. But there had to be one bold one out of the group.

Shawn

Out of all days, this bitch would pick today to start some shit. Knowing my girl was spending the night with me, I was geeked the fuck up. Sexing her in the car was one thing, but knowing I'd be hitting that in a bed all damn night was something totally different.

"Shawn, why haven't I heard from you?" Kanadra walked up and asked.

"Shorty, go on with that shit. You see me with my girl. Beat ya feet," I told the girl and threw my arm around Quaysha.

Kanadra was a chick I bussed down a few times before Quaysha stopped being stingy with the pussy. Her pussy was mediocre, but her head game was on PhD level, and I meant that shit. I'd fucked with a lot of girls—most of them my brother and I tag teamed—but none of them had a mouth piece like that damn Kanadra. But that's all she was good for, and she damn sure ain't had shit on my girl.

Quaysha, though some considered homely, was freaking gorgeous. Add that to the fact that her body was sick, and she was smart as hell, I had the perfect female. She was super smart, and being a virgin was the added bonus in my book. A whole foot shorter than me with big ass tits, no waist, hair to the middle of her back, big Bambi eyes, and a fat ass, she had a nigga gone. The only issue I had was she didn't see what I saw. She was meek and thought nothing of herself. Let her tell it, she was some ugly duckling. If she only knew, she was the topic of plenty locker room discussions.

"Oh, but you wasn't saying that when you was shooting ya kids down my throat a month ago," Kanadra said, stopping both me and Quaysha in our tracks. Quaysha looked up at me, and I could see the hurt in her eyes, begging me to tell her it wasn't true.

I removed my arm from Quaysha and walked up to Kanadra so fast, she didn't have time to process what I was getting ready to do. Grabbing her up by her neck with both hands, I loudly whispered, "Bitch, if you ever in your fucking life say some disrespectful shit like that again around my girl, I promise they'll find you floating somewhere. Now try me."

She was gasping for air, but I didn't give a shit. Quaysha's voice is the only thing that made me drop the ho where she stood.

"Shawn, please stop. Please! You're hurting her!" Quaysha all but yelled. And this why she had my heart. Regardless of the fact this chick just stood here and said my dick was down her throat, Quaysha was concerned about her wellbeing.

Once I let her down, she said, "I'm sorry. I didn't mean it. I-I-I was lying, Quaysha. I'm sorry."

I stood behind Quaysha and winked at Kanadra, glad that she had found some damn sense.

"Oh my God, Shawn. I thought you were going to kill her." Baby girl had tears in her eyes, and it tugged at my heart.

"I'm sorry, ma. She pissed me off so bad. That was disrespectful, and I didn't want you believing no shit like that." She brushed the side of my face with her hand before embracing me, laying her head on my chest.

What Quaysha didn't know was that I would beat a bitch's ass as quick as I would a nigga's. She never had to worry about seeing that side of me because she wasn't the type of female to deserve it. I vowed when I got with her, I would never put my hands on her. Honestly, I didn't want to put my hands on any female, but it was a learned behavior. My father put his hands on my mother, and she loved that nigga's dirty drawers. Dreek stayed putting his foot up a female's ass, and it seemed the more he beat 'em, the more they loved him. Some females were just so damn weak. But I knew regardless of how docile Quaysha was, that wasn't the type of treatment she deserved.

After she got herself together, we walked hand in hand

into the school. Every time I looked down into Quaysha's eyes, I could see the love she had for me. Yeah, I fucked up and hit a chick or two every now and then since we'd been together, but this girl was really my heart and soul. I couldn't see myself without her.

***

"That was a great game, babe. *Four* touchdowns in the first half, and *three* in the second? Is anyone else on the team? I mean, colleges are going to start looking at you soon, if they aren't already," Quaysha said as she laid on my chest while I ran my hands through her hair. She stayed boosting a nigga's head up after the games, and I loved it.

I had something special planned for her tonight. Little did she know, her whole world was going to change. Everything as she knew it before tonight would be a thing of the past... literally.

She removed herself from laying on my chest and looked into my eyes.

"Why me, Shawn? Out of all the girls you could have chosen, why me?" she asked. Instead of telling her how she was the boys' topic of discussion and how banging her body was, I spoke from the heart.

"Quay... you different from all these other girls. You're smart, humble, you stay to yourself, come from a good family, and you ride for ya man. You're my up when I'm down. When school and this football shit gets to me, you're my voice of reasoning. Don't take this crazy when I say it, but you know how I feel about my moms. I look at her as being this weak ass female that lets a man run all over her because she has nothing to offer in return. It's not like that wit' you.

They say a man is attracted to a female that reminds him of his mother, but I beg to differ. You're the exact opposite of her. Regardless of how you view yourself, I see you as beautiful and strong with more to offer than I deserve. You don't crowd a nigga, you give me my space, and it doesn't matter how I feel about a situation, if you feel just as strong about it, you're gonna stand up for yourself. I respect and admire that." I paused and got up

82

off the bed to reach in my dresser drawer.

When I turned around, you could see the look of shock on Quaysha's face as her hand flew up to her mouth and tears began pouring from her eyes.

"We're young, Quaysha, I know this. But I also know I could not see myself with anyone else other than you. You are the true definition of a queen. I know we can't right now, but once we're able..." I got down on one knee and opened the box, revealing a half-carat diamond ring that I'd been saving up for. "...will you marry me?"

The tears continued to flow as she shook her head from side to side. For a minute, I was nervous because I thought she was saying no.

"Yes, Shawn. I'll marry you. Oh my God! Yes, I'll marry you!" she screamed, prompting both Keyonna and Dreek to bust in the room half naked. Hell, we were too, but after I slid the ring on her finger, that didn't stop her from getting up, jumping into Keyonna's arms, and them jumping around and around in circles.

"Bestieeeee, I'm so happy for you!" Keyonna screamed.

Dreek walked over to me and shook his head but dapped me up.

"I didn't really think you were going to go through with it. You sure you wanna do this?" he asked, and I knew why he asked. Hell, it was just three weeks ago I was smashing other females, but I knew who had my heart, and I refused to let another dude have her.

"I'm sure, man. I got this."

"Aight, bruh. Well, congratulations then. Oh, she gon' go get emancipated?" he asked, causing both Keyonna and Quaysha to look in our direction. I could see the worry spread across Quaysha's face, and that was the last thing I wanted.

"I didn't think about that, Shawn. Umm, we can just wait until I'm eighteen," she said, and I agreed. But evidently, Dreek had other plans.

"Nah. If you can get your parents to agree, you can

84

move in here with Shawn, and y'all can start y'all life together now. Or... you can always do something to get kicked out, and that will force the courts to emancipate you sooner. It's up to you though, baby girl. I just want you to know I don't have a problem with you living here," he said.

Hell, we were only fifteen... well, I was getting ready to be sixteen next month, but still, we were young as fuck. Quaysha didn't even know what I did to get money, but if she moved in, she would for damn sure find out, and I didn't know if she would agree with it.

I cut my eyes at Dreek and then nodded to the direction of the bag that was in the corner. He looked at it then back at me and squinted his eyes, and I dropped my head which was all the confirmation he needed to know that she wasn't aware of my current 'occupation.' He nodded his head in understanding before shrugging, grabbing Keyonna, and walking back out the door.

"Look, babe, don't worry about that right now. The only thing I want you to focus on is knowing that you and I will have a life together, whether it be now, a year from now, or ten years from now. Either way, you will be Mrs. Shawn Rivers, you hear me?"

She smiled brightly before jumping on me, wrapping her legs around my waist, and sticking her tongue as far down my throat as it would go. Needless to say, we celebrated our engagement by fucking up some sheets until the sun came up.

Until it wasn't

Six months later

Shawn

"Ahh, shit. Suck that shit, Nadra!" I had Kanadra over at the crib giving me some of the best head in the fuckin' world. Quay and I were still together, but ever since she lost our baby, she was on some other shit. She didn't wanna fuck, and she would never give me head, so that was out of the question.

When her parents found out she was pregnant, they kicked her out, and of course, she ended up moving in with me. I didn't have a problem with it, but when she found out I was a jack boy, she almost lost her shit. I had never seen that side of her before, but for real, I low key thought I was going to have to beat her ass for how she was coming off at me. She was mad as hell. She even blamed the stresses of what I was doing in the streets to be the cause of her miscarriage. I wasn't going to say it wasn't possible, but I highly doubted it.

So since she wasn't putting out and had an attitude about everything under the sun for the past month, every time her ass stayed after school with the debate team, Kanadra was over here getting her back blown out.

"Don't move. I'm finna... I'm finna... cummmm. Arrrggghhhh!" Her nasty ass swallowed my seeds and continued sucking until she got me back up. I knew that only meant she wanted me up in them guts, and I didn't have a problem obliging.

Kanadra got on all fours and tooted her ass up in the air—the way I loved to look at her. She wasn't an ugly girl, but she wasn't a dime. She was average. Where she lacked in looks, she made up for it with her head and shape, because the ass I was staring at right now put my fiancée's to shame, and my fiancée had one of the biggest asses at the school.

After sliding on a condom, I spread her ass cheeks open, slowly sliding my dick into her asshole. I'd convinced her to let me try this a while back, and once we started, we both were hooked. The last time my brother and I had run a train on this girl, he was in her back door while I was in the front, and he always said that shit felt like heaven. He wasn't lying.

"Mm, aaaaah, Shawnnnn! Dammmmmmnnnn!" Kenadra screamed out once I started pounding in and out of her. Between her screams and watching the ripples in her ass, I knew it wasn't going to be any time before I busted another nut. Just as I was getting ready to cum, the room door flew open, and who walked in fucked my head up.

Quaysha and Keyonna stood at the door, and the tears were welling up in Quaysha's eyes. *Damn. I done fucked up*, I thought to myself. Keyonna shook her head as the tears Quaysha had been holding back fell down her pretty face.

"Y'all gon' stand there and look or close the door!

Damn!" Kenadra had the nerve to say. My dick was still in her ass when her head hit the headboard before her body was being dragged from the bed.

"Bitch... you... thought... this... shit... was... what... you... wanted! I... warned... you... it's... not!" Between each word Quaysha spoke, she bombarded Kenadra's face with punches. And here I stood with a semi-hard dick, not knowing what the hell to do next.

"Quaysha, baby, stop!" I finally yelled out, attempting to grab her.

"I wish the *fuck* you would touch me, you shit on the dick ass nigga! I promise to God and twelve other black men, if you put your fucking hands on me, I will cut yo' shit off!" she yelled with Kenadra's hair in her hand, yanking on it with each syllable.

No lie—I believed her. But at the same time, threatening me wasn't the move. I didn't give a fuck that she'd caught me balls deep in some ass... literally.

I ran up on her and grabbed her by the shirt. "You better

pipe the fuck down, and remember who you talking to, bitch. And if you think about leaving, I swear to God, I'll see you in a body bag first," I said through gritted teeth. Keyonna's heads spun around quickly.

"I know damn well you ain't just call my girl no bitch and threaten her, Shawn. Please tell me you didn't," Keyonna said.

I looked at Quaysha with a scowl on my face, but all that bass she had in her voice a second ago didn't match the look on her face currently bore. The tears began spilling from her eyes once again as she released the grip she had on Kenadra's hair and I released the grip on her shirt, and she backpedaled out of the room. Keyonna looked at me and shook her head before following her girl out. Once I heard the front door slam, I looked outside my window, and sure enough, they were pulling off.

I turned back around and looked at Kenadra. Shorty's face was beat the hell up, but that ain't had shit to do with her ass. Deciding to stroke her feelings a little bit so I could finish getting my nut, I sweet talked her some.

91

"Come here, baby." I gently grabbed her up by the arm and sat her back on the bed then walked to the kitchen to get an Ziploc bag with some ice and a washcloth from the bathroom. Once I had it to where I could feel the effects of the ice through the rag, I went back in the room and put it up against her the left side of her face, which was swollen the most. She must have needed to get her off as well because she hadn't made an attempt to put her clothes back on.

While she was trying to stop the swelling, my hands found their way between her legs. I eased two fingers in at first before stopping at three. She was dripping wet and had put the rag down with ice and was now laid back on the bed, fiddling with her nipples.

"Fuck me, Shawn," she said.

For a moment, I kinda felt something for shorty, but the shit didn't last long when I went up in her, and after four deep, long strokes, she was as wide as the Pacific Ocean. Good thing, 'cause a nigga had run up in it bareback. Reaching over in my nightstand drawer to grab another condom, I gestured for her to get back on her knees with that ass tooted up in the air. Within seconds, my dick had found the tightness of her asshole once again, and everything that happened a moment prior was a memory for both of us.

Quaysha

I rode around with Keyonna for an hour, in tears. I couldn't believe I had just walked in on Shawn having sex with the same female he choked out for disrespecting me. Then, to top it all off, *he* disrespected me in front of her.

"Girl, dry your tears. Leave Shawn's ass the hell alone. Beg your parents to come back home, and forget the day Shawn Rivers ever entered your life," Keyonna said, stealing glances at me while trying to keep her eyes on the road.

"I can't, Key. My parents are not going to let me come back home. You know when I called them after I lost the baby, they hung up on me, so something as simple as

Shawn sleeping with another female definitely is not going to make them want to speak to me."

"Simple? Do you hear yourself? Not only did this nigga sleep with another female, he was fucking her in the ass, Quay. *In the ass!* Has he ever fucked you in the a—"

"Oh my God! Don't you dare say it. I would never let any man violate me like that, and you know it! And I wasn't saying it as the act itself was simple, Key. I was saying that in their minds, if their only child losing her child didn't make them want to have a conversation with me, then their child's 'fiancé' sleeping with another female definitely isn't," I told her.

By no means did I think what Shawn had done was acceptable. Oh, I knew better. But, what I was getting ready to tell Keyonna was definitely going to have her looking at me in a different way, and I didn't want that. If I never needed her, I needed her more than anything right now. Before I could say anything else, she started speaking.

"So when did Shawn start calling you out of your

94

name?" she asked as she parked the car. We were at McDonald's, where the majority of the kids came after school. It was pretty much cleared out though since it was going on five o'clock.

I dropped my head because I knew what I was getting ready to tell my best friend would change her outlook on Shawn and possibly end her relationship with Dreek.

"Umm... it started the month after I moved in. I found out what he did for a living one night when he and Dreek came home, talking loudly, and they thought I was asleep. Evidently, they had went to some upscale neighborhood in Lexington. I don't know why he thought I was sleep because they had been gone all day."

"I remember that weekend. Dreek told me he had some business to tend to out of town. But go 'head. Finish."

"Well, I overheard Dreek fussing at Shawn because he said he'd almost gotten them caught. They came home with a thirty thousand dollars, Key. Dreek said they could have gotten a hundred thousand had Shawn not been so stupid.

Instead of me keeping quiet, I jumped out of the bed and ran in the living room. I knew I startled them because they both looked like deer caught in headlights. But instead of Shawn trying to explain the situation, he instantly went in, calling me all kinds of nosy bitches and said he hated that my dumb ass moved in with him. I thought Dreek would come to my defense, but he stood there, nodding his head, and then said, 'that's right. Check her, bruh.'"

I didn't even want to look at Key after I told her that. I was too embarrassed.

"And what else? You're holding back. What the fuck else happened, Quaysha?" Keyonna was light skinned, and her face had turned fire truck red, so I knew she was piping hot.

"Umm... well, he raped me that night. I told him I didn't want to have sex with him, and I wanted to go home, bu-bu-but he raped me, Key!" I screamed out. Just thinking about it broke my heart all over again.

I expected Keyonna to try and comfort me, but she didn't. When I looked up at her, she had tears streaming down her face, but her expression was stoic and unreadable. Suddenly, she started banging on the steering wheel, which caught me off guard.

"You are taking yo' ass home. Do you hear me? I don't want to hear shit about your parents not accepting you. You are going home."

"You don't understand... Key... I umm... umm... We got married, Key. I'm so sorry," I said, reaching for her, but she yanked away from me. The hurt in her eyes could not be missed, but it did nothing to match the hurt in my heart from not only what I'd experienced today knowing that I'd hurt my best friend as well.

"It's gonna get worse, Quay. Don't you see that? Niggas like Shawn don't change. First it starts with verbal abuse, and then the verbal turns into him putting hands on you. I refuse to bury my sister. Please... if you don't do anything else, at least promise to tell someone else. Seek help, Quay, before it's too late," she said then finally grabbed me and held me, rocking back and forth. I knew she was right, but I loved my *husband*.

***

"Attention, students and staff. This is Principal Williams. The school is now on a mandatory lockdown. Teachers, please do not allow students to leave the classrooms. Teachers, I repeat, please do not allow students to leave the classroom," the principal's voice announced over the intercom.

I was locked in the bathroom with my cell phone and a gun. I had called up to the school and threatened to end my life. Two black eyes and a broken... yet I was four months pregnant by a man that vowed to love me. If this was love, I was over it.

When I first went to one of the counselors at the school like Keyonna suggested, I was told that since Shawn and I were married, they highly doubted the police would do anything about the verbal abuse. This same administrator went back and told Shawn that I came to the office, complaining. Not only did he beat me black and blue when he came home that day, but he also let me listen to the

98

recording of them having sex in her office. From there, the beatings were at least once a month until they started coming once a week. Finding out I was pregnant again stopped him, but once we found out last week that we were having a girl, the beatings started up again. He beat me so bad Sunday that I ended up in the hospital. Had he come with me, knowing I would have lied for him, he would have found out that the ultrasound tech made an error, and we were actually having a boy.

I was released from the hospital yesterday, and instead of going home to him, I walked the streets all night and found an unlocked abandoned car to sleep in. Anything was better than going home to him. This morning when I woke up, I knew he would think I was still in the hospital, so I took the chance of going by the house. I thanked God Dreek wasn't home. After I retrieved his gun from under the mattress where he didn't know I knew he kept it, I bathed and made my way to school, sore but mostly broken. But the broken I was experiencing, no doctor could heal.

Hearing someone enter the bathroom, I quickly put one

in the chamber and aimed my gun. I was going to end my life, but whoever was stupid enough to come in here was dying with me. My only regret was not being able to bring the life I created into this world. Regardless of what Shawn and I were going through, somewhere deep down, I know that my son was conceived from love.

"Quay... Quay, sis, it's me." Keyonna entered the bathroom with her hands raised in the air. My hands trembled uncontrollably. I knew I wasn't going to pull the trigger on my best friend, but I also knew she wouldn't let me end my own life.

"Key, go away, please! Just go away!"

When she stepped closer to me and saw my face, her hands covered her mouth as she covered a scream.

"Oh my God, Quay. Look at you... Why are you allowing yourself to go through this? Sis, please, let me help you. You're pregnant with my niece. You can't keep going through this," she said, sobbing as she inched closer to me.

"Actually... I'm having a boy. The ultrasound tech made a mistake," I informed her, dropping my head along with the gun. It seemed as if as soon as I did that, police swarmed in the bathroom, but Key held on to me tightly. In that moment... I decided I wanted to live.

Why me?

Four years later

Quaysha

"OK. I will make sure dinner is done and that I confirm my aunt is still going to keep Junior before I leave for work," I said before disconnecting the call.

Over the years, I had started rebuilding a relationship with some members in my family, my aunt in particular. When she found out that I was pregnant and being abused, she vowed to keep my secret and help out in any way she could. And though the abuse with Shawn had slowed down tremendously, the fact that my son has seen his father put his hands on me, does not sit well with me.

"I don't understand how after all these years, you still continue to put up with his mess. Look at you. You're a beautiful girl with so much going for yourself, yet you choose to settle for... that," my best friend Keyonna said as I put the finishing touches on her hair.

102

Keyonna was the only person I'd confided in during my high school years about the abuse I was enduring. When I got pregnant and left my parents' house, it was sort of like experiencing my first heartbreak. My father was the first man to ever tell me he loved me. Yet he was the first man to turn his back on me. I always felt like if maybe he wouldn't have put me out just to keep his name from being tarnished, maybe, just maybe I wouldn't have endured the hell I'd gone through with Shawn.

"Girl, I got a plan. I'm leaving Shawn. I actually got approved for housing last week, and with this raise and new managerial position at Family Dollar, I don't have to depend on him anymore. I've also decided to tell my family about what's been going on."

Her head spun around so fast, I almost burned her with the curling iron.

"Thank God! Going to school and working has given the scarecrow a brain! That's what I'm talkin' about!" She laughed, and I rolled my eyes but joined in on the laughter. I was ecstatic that things were finally looking up for me, and I no longer had to endure dealing with Shawn and his abuse. He was in for a rude awakening, because come next week, my son and I would be gone.

Keyonna stood up as I handed her the handheld mirror for her to look at the back of her hair.

"Yeeeessss, boo. This is exactly how I wanted it." She went in her purse to pay me, but I placed my hand on top of hers.

"No—not this time. You've done enough. Just keep Junior for me next week while I get my keys, and ask your brother if he knows anyone that will help me move the few things that I do have, and that is repayment enough," I told her.

"Umm, you sure? 'Cause you know I ain't about to beg you to take my money," she questioned with her hand on her hip.

"I bet you ain't, but I'm sure. And thank you so much for everything. I'll call you in the morning when I wake up, OK?"

"Alright, love," she replied before walking over to the couch and kissing Shawn Jr. on the forehead. I followed her to the door and gave her a quick hug before locking up behind her. Shawn couldn't stand Keyonna, and though he knew she was here, I made sure that she was never in his presence for long. Once I returned to the kitchen, I removed the chicken breasts from the refrigerator, grabbed the rice and Sazón from the cabinet, and got a bag of broccoli out the freezer to start dinner. Though I knew cooking a full meal before I went to work was going to have me tired, I did it to avoid hearing Shawn's mouth.

Four hours later

I was already off to a bad start. This would be my second time being late as a manager, and that just didn't look good. My aunt couldn't keep my son, and Shawn decided his ass just wasn't going to come home to get him, so now I was running around trying to find a babysitter at the last moment. It was 4:15, and I was supposed to be to work in fifteen minutes, which was damn near impossible.

105

Out of options, I gave in and decided to call my mother.

I let the phone ring four times and was about to hang up when she finally answered.

"Good afternoon, Merritt's residence."

"Umm, hey, Ma."

"Quaysha... what can I do for you?" she asked in a snobbish tone that immediately made me regret calling her.

"I'm running late for work, and Aunt Bobbi said she couldn't keep Junior for me today because something important came up. I was wondering if you could keep him for me this one time. I'm a manager now, and I don't want to mess this up. It's really important to me, Ma."

Silence met me on the other end of the line. I heard her let out a long sigh before saying, "OK. You can bring him. Make sure—"

"I know damn well you wasn't about to take my son over to that bitch. The fuck is wrong wit' you!" Shawn yelled, snatching my phone from my hand.

"I have to be to work in five minutes, Shawn, and my au—"

WHAP!

"I don't give a fuck about all of that!"

I prayed the slap would be the only lick he administered, but my prayers went unanswered. Shawn Jr. screamed at the top of his lungs while Shawn yanked me by my hair, pulled me to the ground, and dragged me down the hallway, punching me as if I was a ragdoll. I could have cried. The average female would have cried. But I had no more tears left.

Once we reached the room, he picked me up and threw me on the bed, delivering a swift hard punch to my face. I knew there was no way I could go to work this evening and possibly not for the next few days. Shawn had gotten better about not leaving marks on my face, only giving me body shots, but today was different. *He* was different. He yanked my khaki pants down, ripping them in the process, and was about to do the same to my panties. The ringing of his cell phone halted his actions.

"Bitch, what!" he screamed at the person on the other end. "I told you, that's not my fuckin' seed you carryin'. Don't call my damn line again until you produce some damn DNA results!" he yelled and threw the phone on the floor. Oh, so that was the problem? He had some random pregnant and couldn't deal with that, and instead of handling the situation like the man he was supposed to be—the one he always claimed he was—he was here, taking it out on me.

For the next twenty minutes, Shawn violated all of my holes, but I was so numb both physically and emotionally, all I could do was lay there. The only reason the tears began to fall down my face was because I had to sit there and listen to my three-year-old pound on the door, his soft voice screaming, "Daddy, please stop hurting Mommy! Stop, Daddy, stop!" That broke my heart more than anything Shawn was doing to me at the moment.

After he finished beating and raping me, he had the audacity to shower and leave. My son lay on the floor on the other side of the bedroom door, with a tear-stained face. He had cried himself to sleep, and it killed me that I was

108

allowing him to witness this. At that moment, I knew what I had to do. I picked his little body up, as sore as I was, and placed him in the bed then grabbed my cell phone.

"Mommy, please tell Daddy I'm on my way, and I need to speak with y'all. Umm... Shawn has been abusing me since eleventh grade..."

Six months later

Things were going great. It was rough juggling school, work, and being a single mom, but with the help of my parents, other family members, and Keyonna, I was managing. I had even started back going to church and renewing my faith. I hadn't seen Shawn since that day he almost made me lose my job, and in a way, I thank God for what he did that day. It gave me the strength to walk away.

He'd been calling and leaving little threatening messages here and there, saying he was going to kill me if he ever saw me, but after the first couple of messages along with the police report from that day, I was able to get an order of protection. He was not allowed to come anywhere near me.

Many times, I thought back on how crazy I was to stay with him for so long. I mean, Shawn had my mind so gone, I would call the school and issue bomb threats because I'd be locked in one of the bathrooms contemplating suicide. That man really did a number on me, and I didn't think I

110

would ever be able to give anyone else my heart.

My lunch break was over, and I was headed back out front to deal with the last wave of customers. I couldn't wait to get home and see my little fat man. Keyonna had moved in with me, and we split the bills fifty-fifty. The days she didn't work, she would keep Junior for me.

"Alright, Sonya. I'll see you bright and early tomorrow," I told one of the employees whose shift was over. After ringing up the last customer, I locked up the doors and turned off the overhead lights in front of the store to indicate we were closed.

"Trent, I didn't even know you worked closing tonight. That's a shame since I'm the one that made the schedule," I said and laughed.

"Yeah. I'm glad I did. I don't like when you have to work to closing by yourself. You too pretty; someone might snatch you up."

I blushed and laughed lightly. Trent, like most of the male employees, had a little crush on me, which I thought was cute. None of them ever made the attempt to cross the line with me which showed me they did respect me enough to know it would never happen. Trent was a little cutie though.

"Aww, I'm a big girl. I can handle myself," I told him as I finished depositing the money from the drawer into the safe so I could do a bank run in the morning.

"Alright, all set. Ready to go?"

"After you," Trent said, holding the door open like a true gentleman.

On the way to our cars, which were actually across the street from the store since we allowed the customers full access to the parking lot in front of the store, we laughed about one of the customers that came in the store on the regular.

"Yo, what the fuck!" Trent yelled.

When I turned my head, there stood Shawn with a smirk on his face and pistol in hand.

"So you still leaving me? For this nigga, Quay? Huh? For this nigga?"

"Shawn, I'm not leaving you for anyone. This is my employee," I said, trying my hardest to defuse the situation. Even in minimal lighting, I could tell that Shawn had been drinking. His eyes were bloodshot red, and his words were slurring.

"You ain't nothing but a fuckin' ho, and that's why I treated you as such. Ain't been gone for but a few months, and you already caking with the next dude!" Shawn was fuming, but I stood there in shock and confused.

"Shawn, please, put the gun down."

"Nigga, you ain't gotta fuckin' talk to he—"

POW! POW!

"Oh my God, Shawn, what have you done!"

He looked up at me with the coldest eyes I'd ever seen as he began walking toward.

"Bitch, I always told you, the only way you was

113

leaving was in a body bag. I'm a man of my word."

POW! POW! POW!

****

"This is Tina Benton with breaking news out of Lancaster, South Carolina. I am at the Family Dollar on Great Falls Road where there was a double homicide. A Mr. Shawn Rivers was still at the scene holding the murder weapon when police arrived. We are still trying to gather the details... OK... OK... It seems the bodies were identified as twenty-one-year-old, Quaysha Merritt, and twenty-four-year-old, Trent Davis. Merritt was one of the managers at..."

About the Author

Sparkle Lewis, whose real name is Latisha Burns, was born in Brooklyn, New York, and currently resides in Fayetteville, North Carolina. She is a wife and mother of four. Her love for writing began as early as elementary school when she started writing poems for her friends. As she got older, this fascination with writing turned into reading urban fiction, and she started working on her first novel, which to date is still unpublished.

On January 1, 2018, she signed a contract with Major Key Publishing. In addition to being an author, Latisha is a ghostwriter and also the owner of Touch of Class Publishing Services LLC, which provides editing and proofreading services to multiple publishing companies in the industry. Other titles in her collection include *They Can't Stop Me: Return of a Savage*, *Unconditional Hood Love*, and *Ki'Asia: Queen City's Finest* parts 1 and 2.

Dying For Your Love

By Christina Fletcher

Synopsis

After a failed marriage, Jade is a single mother and nurse who's looking for love. She becomes so desperate that she's willing to date a married man, Dwayne. Jade doesn't think twice about it because he assures her that he's in the middle of a divorce. Things go well in their relationship for a while, until Dwayne starts showing his true colors. She soon realizes she's in for way more than she bargained for.

Morgan is married to who once was the love of her life, Tyler. He has changed a lot over the course of their marriage and has become dangerously abusive. For some reason, she's willing to keep enduring because she believes he'll eventually change. It's not until she experiences a life-altering event that lands her in the hospital, and she decides enough is enough. She has a real eye-opening experience when she meets her nurse, Jade, and feels empowered to let Tyler go once and for all.

Chapter 1 Jade

High school diploma. College degree. Get married. Start a family. That was the typical American Dream, but plans get thrown off, and Lord knows it didn't always happen the way we wanted it to. What happened to actually falling in love and marrying your soulmate? What happened to a husband loving his wife and a wife honoring and submitting to her husband? I thought I was doing everything right since I did things in what I thought was the right order, but I guess not. Did I fall in love? Yes. Was he my soulmate? Apparently not.

I was in love with Antonio, and I thought our marriage was going great. He treated me like a queen, and I was constantly on cloud nine. However, it was all short-lived because it seemed that after our daughter was born, things began to change. The marriage vows we took went straight out the window after I discovered his infidelity. I stayed and forgave him time and time again, but eventually, it got old. By the time our daughter turned three, our divorce was finalized, and I was ready for new beginnings. The fucked-up part was that Antonio did a 180 on me. Even when he cheated, he still acted like he loved me, but the second I filed for a divorce, he didn't give a shit about breaking my heart, and started flaunting different women around St. Louis. I got tired of the phone calls from different people telling me they saw Antonio with a new bitch every other day.

The only good part about the divorce was that I got to keep our three-bedroom house in Ferguson, Missouri and the Lexus ES and Dodge Charger. All he got was the Honda Accord and had to pay $850 a month in child support. Originally, he was ordered to pay $1,200 for both child support and spousal support, but I made good money as a registered nurse, and I refused to be his charity case. All I cared about was him participating in taking care of our daughter financially, but also physically and emotionally by actively being a part of her life. It was hard at first because we always bumped heads, but we finally figured the co-parenting thing out.

"You ready, baby?" Dwayne called out to me, startling me from my thoughts.

"Yeah, baby, I am," I replied.

I sat at my vanity and finished applying my makeup. We were heading out to see that movie *Get Out*. I heard it was good, so I was looking forward to seeing it and catching dinner at Landry's afterward.

I had been dating Dwayne for about three months now, and so far, things were going well. Dwayne was also in the medical profession and told me he had a career as a speech-language pathologist. I really liked him, but I also wanted to take things as slowly as possible because I was guarding my heart. I finally gave him some pussy a couple of weeks ago though. We'd only been intimate twice, but I liked feeling in control and doing things on my terms. He seemed OK with that, and he didn't have any objections to anything. We still had a few kinks to work out between us, but that was nothing and wouldn't stop us from progressing.

"Come on, bae, so we won't be too late. I don't want those up-close seats we'll get stuck with if we arrive after the movie start, because I don't like stretching my neck," he said.

"Believe me, I don't either," I replied, laughing.

He smiled, flashing me those perfect pearly whites. Dwayne was fine as hell as he stood almost six feet tall with caramel colored skin. He wore his hair cut low with a nice trimmed up goatee. His voice was Barry White deep, and it mesmerized me every time he spoke. I got up from my vanity, he helped me put my jacket on, and we headed out the front door.

It was a warm night for early March, and we rode with the windows down. I was enjoying the cool breeze and vibing to Ledisi's "Pieces of Me" he had blasting out of the speakers. I closed my eyes, snapped, and bobbed my head, just enjoying the moment. Dwayne grabbed my hand, intertwining his fingers in mine. I opened my eyes, looked at him, and smiled. He brought my hand to his lips and kissed it softly. I felt myself melting into the leather seats of his Buick Lacrosse. After Antonio, I never thought any man would make me feel this way again. I felt beautiful and liked, being someone's woman.

"I really enjoy spending time with you, Jade," Dwayne said.

"I like spending time with you too," I replied.

"I look forward to seeing where things go with us."

"I do too."

This moment seemed so surreal for some reason. We continued to ride down Washington Avenue in silence, on our way to the MX Movie Theater downtown. The song switched to Boyz II Men's "I'll Make Love to You", and I knew I was going to give him some pussy again tonight. Everything felt just right in this moment, and listening to this song made me think about the couple of times we did make love. He pulled up to the front of the theater right before the song ended and let me out so he could drive around to find a parking space.

"I'll see you inside in a minute," he said.

"Yep. I'll go ahead and grab the tickets," I told him.

"You know I was paying, right?" he replied.

"Nope. I have it tonight," I said.

"I don't like the idea of that, but I won't argue with you. I'll pay for dinner then," he responded.

"Fair enough," I said with a wink.

Right before I climbed out the car, the music was interrupted by his ringing phone. Since he had it connected to the Bluetooth in the car, I could see the name and number flash across the radio screen. The name "My Wife" lit the car up in blue light. I cut him a look, but there was nothing I could say, because I already knew the deal. I just climbed out of the car and closed the door as he answered her call. As he drove away, I could hear her voice come out over the speakers since the windows were still cracked.

"Where are you at, and when are you coming in?" I heard her ask.

Of course, I couldn't hear his response. I didn't know why it made me jealous anytime she called. I knew he was married from the beginning and in the middle of a divorce. He told me that sometimes he still went by there and stayed the night sometimes because the divorce was really hard on their two children. He slept in the guest room and usually left for work as the children left out for school. I figured it was only fair he did that because I saw first-hand how hard my and Antonio's divorce was on Alicia. I decided to call my mother to check in on my daughter before I became too occupied with my date. I just hoped he told his wife he would be in really late or not at all because I was planning on busting it wide open for him tonight.

Chapter 2 Morgan

My jaws were hurting hella bad. I kept sucking though, making sure to tighten my jaws and drag my lip hard enough but not too hard so I wouldn't bite him. I made slurping noises, hoping to turn him on even more than he already was. He lied flat on his back, lifted his right leg at his knee, grabbed my head, and began fucking my mouth back. It used to turn me on when he would get excited about me giving him head. That excitement eventually became disappointment because I never seemed to get my nut afterward. I figured there was no point in wasting good pussy juice by getting worked up for nothing. I still wanted to get him as aroused as I could though so he would go ahead and cum, and I could go to bed.

"Get this nut up out of me," Tyler said through gritted teeth.

He kept tensing up, so I could tell that he was about ready to cum. I kept at it, even though my neck had started hurting now too. He grabbed a fist full of my hair and jabbed his dick further into my throat. I wasn't good at deep throating, but I wanted to please him, so I did my best to loosen up and relax. My eyes watered, and I began to gag, but all it did was turn him on even more. I felt a sense of relief when I looked toward his feet and noticed his toes began to curl.

"There it go, baby. That… nut… about… to…," he said, as his cum shot to the back of my throat.

I swallowed it, wiping the excess spit off my mouth with the back of my hand. I lied down on my back and began to stare at the ceiling. He pulled me close, and he kissed my cheek.

"I love you, baby," he said.

"I love you too," I replied dryly.

I was feeling horny, but our sex always ended the same way, with him feeling satisfied and me still feeling sexually frustrated. I was getting tired of playing with my clit when he wasn't around just so I could cum. I did everything this man asked me to do from licking all over his body, sucking his toes, and giving him head whenever he wanted it. I was lucky if I got head once a month, but that was after I damn near had to beg or ask for it about ten times. If he did give in, he did it with an attitude. He'd usually ignore me though or busy himself with something else like watching TV or smoking a cigarette. Sometimes, he'd say he was sleepy and to let him rest a few minutes before he got up to do it. He usually never did though because when I'd try to wake him after a few minutes, he'd yell at me about how tired he was or say he had a headache.

I eventually just stopped asking him to perform oral sex on me because pleasuring myself had become my normal routine. I'd sometimes ask for his help by asking him to suck my titties or even just play with my nipples while I stroked my clit, but he acted like that was hard work too. I just gave up on getting an orgasm with him altogether and would just wait for him to go take a shower or leave for work before I finished myself off. I was getting tired of this, and he knew it too; he just didn't give a shit.

I often fantasized about past lovers and thought about who ate my pussy the best in order to excite myself enough to have an orgasm. My girls and I always swapped sex stories when we got together, and I had to laugh along or pretend I was experiencing the same thing when God knew I was far from getting even half of the pleasure their men gave them. After eight years of marriage, things just seemed to get worse and only seemed to go well as long as I was doing things to please him. I bent over backward for this man, but he never seemed to show me half of the love I showed him. He filled my head with so many false promises, telling me how he was going to eat my pussy every day and make good love to me, but it stopped happening. In the beginning of the relationship, he did, but I guess our honeymoon phase expired, and sex was just something to keep him content whenever he wanted it, because it sure didn't happen on my terms.

"What's wrong?" Tyler asked as if he were really concerned.

I knew telling him would mean absolutely nothing to him, and not telling him would mean I was holding something back from him. Either way, whether I said nothing or told him the truth, he would get upset. I was so used to this that I figured I would have a better way of answering his question by now whenever he asked me what was wrong, but I didn't.

"I'm OK." I sighed, not wanting to feel even more

disappointed by telling him for nothing.

"No you're not," he said, pulling me closer.

I opened my legs, putting my hand on my pearl and began massaging it. I let out a light moan, hoping he'd catch the hint. As usual, he didn't and just kept lying there. I began to move my hips and moan a little louder, but I still didn't get any reaction out of him.

"Baby, can you play with my nipple or suck my titty please?" I asked him.

He didn't respond. I looked over at him, and his eyes were closed. I knew he wasn't sleep that fast. I reached over and grabbed his hand, placing his fingers over my nipple. Again, I didn't get any reaction from him. I let out another sigh.

"Fuck it," I said, turning my back to him.

"Fuck what?" he replied, frustrated.

"You always get yours. The least bit you could do is help me get mine," I said.

"I gotta get up for work in a few hours. You had a nap earlier, I didn't!" he exploded.

I was in no mood for this usual bullshit for him, so

I just got quiet. Tears fell from my eyes, and when I sniffled, I felt him turn his back to me. I was really beginning to dislike this man. I still loved him, but I had already fallen out of love with him. I wanted to get things back to where they used to be for us, but I didn't think he did.

"Tyler, why don't you love me the way I love you?" I asked him.

"Here you go with this shit! If I didn't love you, I wouldn't be here!" he yelled.

"Because I give you my all, loving you hard every single day. I do anything in the world for you. If you're hurt, I hop up to give you pain medicine, I massage your hurting spots, and I make sure you're OK. I make sure to have your dinner ready every evening. Whatever you need, I got you. When you ask for head, that's not a problem, but when I ask you for it or even for you to just play with a nipple, it's a big fucking deal!" I yelled, letting my emotions get the best of me. The tears were falling even more now.

"Man, I'm so sick of this shit," he said, grabbing a

couple of pillows and getting out of the bed.

He went into the living room, and I lied in the bed, continuing to cry. I was tired of feeling this way. One minute our relationship was up, and we were laughing and smiling, and the next minute, it was down. He wasn't even that affectionate toward me anymore, and he acted like he didn't even like to kiss me for real. I got out the bed and went into the living room because I wanted answers.

"Why does our marriage have to be this way, Tyler?" I asked him.

"Like what, Morgan? All you do is cry and complain, no matter what I do. It ain't no pleasing you," he said.

"Because you don't even try. As long as I'm catering to you, it's all good. When I have an ache or pain, you can't even rub my feet or my back. I can't even ask my husband to help me get my issue off, and I shouldn't even have to ask," I said.

"There are plenty of times we had sex and I didn't nut, but I never complain," he replied.

I was quiet for a second, because I didn't know

what to say. I contemplated what he said, but it was bullshit. For the majority, his ass came because he always did in my mouth or he made that high-pitched ass moan when he was inside of me. "So what is it?" I finally asked. "What keeps you from loving me the way that I love you?"

He just shrugged his shoulders.

"Why do I have to beg you for head, but I give you some with no problem?" I asked him.

"I don't know," Tyler replied, looking down at his phone.

"I'm so sick of this," I said, walking away. "Why did you marry me!" I yelled out, slamming the door to our bedroom.

He ran up behind me, busting the bedroom door open. "I'm sick of it too, Morgan! I'm sick of the crying and complaining! I'm sick of you never being happy. That shit brings *me* down!" he yelled.

"Well, just go your way, and I'll go mine. Let somebody come along who will love me, and I can love him back just as hard," I said, hoping to strike a nerve.

"If that's what you want, that's fine," he said, going

to the closet to grab some clothes and began stuffing them in his suitcase. "I'll be out of your house tomorrow."

I lied in bed and kept crying, wondering why things had to be this way. I wasted so much time on him and was just ready to be done with this marriage. It was empty anyway, and it was not like he could do anything for me. I was too busy making sure he was straight all the time, and he didn't even give half a fuck about me.

I must have dozed off without realizing it, because he woke me up, asking me for some money for cigarettes. I looked over at the clock on the end table and saw that it was a quarter to midnight. I closed my eyes and didn't say anything, ignoring him like he did me.

"Man, fuck it," he said, walking out of the room. About two minutes later, he came back in. "So you can't buy me no cigarettes, Morgan?" he asked.

"No. For what? You sick of this and don't wanna do your part in the marriage to keep me happy, so no," I said.

He raised his hand as if he was going to hit me, and I jumped, covering my face.

"Ughhhh," he grunted, balling up his fist. "You're a stupid ass bitch. I hate I ever married your stupid ass. You act like a fucking kid," he said.

"So do you. I spent too much time in this marriage begging you to love me and treat me right. Just let it go. Quit asking me for stuff," I said.

"I'm *not* gon' stop asking, and you're not gon' to stop doing. You said you would always be there, but I guess you lied," he said, getting in my face.

"You lied too, making all those false promises about the way things was going to be between us," I said, closing my eyes and just wanting to go back to sleep.

"So you not gon' buy me no cigarettes?" he asked again, ignoring what I just said.

"No," I replied, with my eyes still closed.

Before I knew it, he had jumped on the bed and began choking me, while he bit my cheek.

"I'm tired of you putting your hands on me!" I could barely scream out because his hands were getting tighter around my neck. He finally stopped biting me cheek and kissed me right where he bit.

"I hate your stupid ass. I hope you die," he said, letting my neck go. I just laid there crying harder and harder. I realized I broke a nail, trying to pry his hands from around my neck. This fool had the nerve to choke me, bite me, then kiss me. I was so damn confused.

A couple of minutes passed before I heard him tell me to come here from outside the door. I knew not to keep ignoring him, so I got out of the bed. He held an ice pack out for me to put to my face. He tried to hold it in place for me, but I told him I had it.

"So you don't want me touching you? Fuck you then," he said. My tears continued to fall. "Take me to get some cigarettes."

"Why can't you take your car and take yourself?" I asked him, handing him my debit card.

"'Cause I want you to take me," he said, walking out the door.

I knew it was no winning, and I didn't want him getting any more upset and hitting me again. I slipped on some shorts and my house shoes and followed behind him like a lost puppy. I drove to the nearest gas station while we rode in silence. I held the ice pack to my face and already knew his bite was going to leave an ugly bruise. When we pulled up, I handed him my debit card so he could get whatever it was he needed to get.

"You get it," he said.

"I have on house shoes, and I'm still holding this ice pack to my face," I replied.

"Man, go get it," he said again, sounding a little frustrated.

Not wanting to piss him off again, I got out the car, set the ice pack on my seat, and closed the door.

"Get a soda too!" he rolled down the window and yelled out.

"What kind?" I asked him softly.

"It don't matter," he said.

I went into the store and got his cigarettes and a Coca-Cola for him. I could see the cashier looking at me with pity, and I hated myself for allowing this mess to continue with Tyler. When I got back into the car, I handed him the bag.

"Thank you," he said.

"You're welcome," I whispered.

"Man, Morgan, look. We gotta get our shit together. We're supposed to be better than this," he said. "We're a team."

"Yeah, we are," I replied, only half listening. I knew this man didn't love me for real, and this was some more temporary bullshit from him in the moment.

"I love you with all of me. I promise I do. You're my world. I don't ever want to hurt you. You just be making me mad with the stupid shit you say sometimes," he said.

"That don't mean you need to put your hands on me," I replied, continuing to speak softly.

"You're right," he said. "I really just be trying to scare you a little bit and let you know who's in charge, not hurt you."

"Why do I have to beg you to love me? Are you not attracted to me anymore?" I asked him. I was already heavyset when we hooked up, and I know I had gained a little more weight since we were married. I shamefully wore a size twenty, and although he always complimented me on how pretty I was, that didn't mean I still turned my husband on.

"Yeah, I'm still attracted to you. I wouldn't have married you. I'm not going to lay in the bed every night with someone I'm not attracted to," he said. "Looks aren't everything though. I've learned to love the one who loves me, and that's why I'm with you, because of how hard you love me."

"So what is it then? Why won't you make love to me the way I make love to you, or why do you turn your nose up when I kiss you?"

"See, you're tripping off stupid stuff, Morgan. You worried about why I turn my nose up and shit like that. If I didn't want to kiss you, I wouldn't. You get upset because I won't kiss you the way *you* want me to. It's not going to always be what *you* want," he said seriously.

"Thing is, it's *never* what I want. I'm always so busy being good to you and giving you what you want, but you don't think about me."

"Man, shit will get better. We just gotta communicate better than we do."

"I do communicate with you and tell you how I feel, but you don't listen."

"You're right. I know I don't communicate with you, and I have to start," Tyler said.

"That would be nice," I replied.

"I love you. I promise I do," he said.

"I love you too, baby."

Deep down, I knew all of this was going to be short-lived because it was the same damn routine we always went through when we got into it or when he put his hands on me. I didn't know why I continued to fall for it or even stay in this marriage, when deep down, I knew it wasn't going to get any better. I really was over it, but there was one thing keeping me from leaving this time. I was pregnant, and I knew he had been trying to get me pregnant forever. I just didn't know if I should leave him and secretly have an abortion or tell him and keep trying to work things out. Maybe he wouldn't hit me anymore since I was pregnant.

When we got back home, we got into the bed and he turned the TV on.

"Can you hold me?" Tyler asked me.

I rolled my eyes, but he didn't see me since the only light in the room was coming from the TV. I wrapped my arms around him and kissed his head.

"You know we're forever, right?" he said.

"Yep. For better or for worse," I replied.

"You ain't going nowhere. If you ever try to leave, I will kill you. I promise to God," he said.

Part of me was thinking *whatever* as I rolled my eyes, but then another part of me believed him because he had put his hands on me way too many times. I closed my eyes, pretending to doze off quickly. I let out a soft snore so he'd stop talking or wouldn't ask me for anything else. That didn't work though.

"Bae?" he said.

"Hmm?" I groaned.

"Can I get some more head?" he asked.

I didn't say anything and pretended like I didn't hear him. I was giving him a dose of his own medicine when he would pretend like he didn't hear me. I waited for a couple of minutes before I faked another light snore. He slipped from my hold, and I opened my eyes. He got out of the bed and grabbed his phone before walking into the living room. Deep down, I already knew he was messing around on me, and that was really what was keeping us from being happy.

Chapter 3 Jade

Dwayne seemed a little irritable on our date the other night after he spoke with his wife. I didn't press the issue because it wasn't really any of my business. I knew I was messing with a married man, and although he said he was divorcing, the reality is that at the end of the day, he was still married. All I could do for now was stay in my lane and let him work through his problems in his own way. I smiled when he walked through the door to join me for lunch at what had become our favorite place to dine. We met here at Café Ventana, and neither of us could seem to stay away from this place.

"How are you today?" I asked him, smiling ear-to-ear.

"I'm doing pretty good. How about yourself?" he asked, leaning across the table to give me a kiss before he sat down.

"I'm as good as to be expected."

"I'm glad to hear that."

"I ordered you the usual. I hope you don't mind."

"Yeah, actually, I do. Next time, just wait for me to

order, and I'll order for myself," he replied a little too sternly. I guess he had an attitude again today. It didn't seem like it at first, but now it did. Then again, maybe I was reading too much into this situation. I just wasn't used to Dwayne acting this way, and it threw me off a little. At least next time I would know to just let the man order his own damn food.

"I'm glad we could meet for lunch since you had to cancel our dinner date later. Is everything OK?" I asked, taking a sip of my water.

He shrugged. "Things are so-so for now. My wife has been tripping about me not spending enough time with the kids, so tonight, I figured I would make it about them."

"I notice you still say *my wife* a lot. For you to be going through a divorce, I figured you'd say your ex or just refer to her by her name," I said, beginning to feel some type of way.

"Well she *is* my wife, so that's what I'ma call her," he said, raising his voice.

I looked around, feeling embarrassed. He didn't seem like himself today. He was normally always so proper and had a professional demeanor all the time. Today, he almost seemed a little too loose and was even letting a little slang come out in his speech, which was also unusual. Again, I didn't want to read too much into things, but my gut was telling me that something wasn't right.

Our food arrived, and he barely touched his plate. I guess he really didn't have a taste for what I ordered for him. I mean, he always ate the same thing, so I don't know why today was different. I knew people got burned out on things sometimes, so maybe that was all it was. I really liked Dwayne, and I didn't want to let the fact that he was having a bad day ruin things. I still appreciated him making time for me today versus canceling on me altogether. I finished my food and asked the waitress for a to-go box. If he wasn't going to eat it, I would damn sure take it home and eat it later. He paid for our meal and walked me to my car.

"I hope we get to spend some more time together soon," I suggested, hoping he'd say after he was finished spending time with his children, or at least tomorrow.

"I'll call you and let you know," he told me.

I wasn't really satisfied with that answer. I sighed. "When will your divorce be final? We've been dating long enough that once your divorce is final, you should be able to bring your kids around me and we all spend time together."

"I will determine when I think we've been dating long enough. Otherwise, don't worry about my divorce. You knew what you were getting into when you started dating me. Now all of a sudden, you're in a rush for things to be final," he said rather coldly. It was like déjà vu. I had been through this before with a man treating me well in the beginning and then suddenly flipping the script. I liked Dwayne a lot, but I didn't know how much longer I would be dealing with him and his situation. I didn't like how he was talking to me right now either.

"Look, I'm sorry I asked. Just call me next time you wanna see me," I purred, hoping that would lighten the mood.

"I told you I would. Drive safe, love," he said.

My heart started racing when he called me love. I knew that didn't necessarily mean anything, but it was still

146

nice to hear. I wrapped my arms around his neck, and right as I was about to kiss him, my cell phone rang. I pulled back so I could reach in my purse to see who it was. A look came across Dwayne's face that I couldn't quite read, but he definitely wasn't happy.

"Hello?" I answered, seeing that it was my ex-husband, Antonio.

"Hey, you. I was calling to let you know that I was going to pick Alicia up for the weekend. That's if it's OK with you," he said.

"Of course." I laughed. "She's *our* daughter. You shouldn't have to ask to get her, but I appreciate your courtesy."

"Alright then. I'll see y'all in a couple of hours around three. Make sure she's ready for a weekend of fun," he said.

"Will do. See you then," I replied.

I hung up my phone and stuffed it back in my purse. Before I could look up, I felt the back of Dwayne's hand connect with my face. I was confused, not sure what hit me at first. It dawned on me within a few seconds as I felt the sting on my cheek, near my eye.

"Dwayne! What the hell! Why are you hitting me!" I screeched.

"Lower your fucking voice," he said through gritted teeth as he wrapped his hands around my neck.

My heart was racing as I tried to pry his hands from around my neck. I struggled to breathe, and I could have sworn my demise was near. He finally let go, and I pulled in gulps of air. I didn't know what had gotten into him, but I was definitely leaving him alone. Was this man on some type of drugs or something? I needed to get away from him and fast too. As if reading my mind, he opened my car door and told me to get in.

"Look, I'm sorry," he said as soon as I sat down.

I didn't say anything but just pulled my seat belt on and looked straight ahead. His apologies didn't mean anything to me right now. All I wanted him to do was close my door and lose my number. I was such a fool to fall for him. I silently prayed that he wouldn't come after me once I called things off. Some people out here were psycho, and I thought I had met one of them.

"So you're just going to ignore me?" he said, raising his voice again. I didn't want to piss him off any more than he was and get hit again, so I looked at him and gave a weak smile.

"I'm just confused, that's all," I whispered. "You were so nice before, and I didn't expect that from you."

"I'm still nice. You just pushed my buttons today, asking about my divorce. On top of that, I felt you were being disrespectful, breaking our hug to talk to your daughter's father. He could have waited."

"I agree," I said, hoping it would defuse the situation, and he would let me drive off. "I'm sorry."

"Just don't let it happen again," he said, kissing the top of my head.

He didn't have to worry about that, because it wouldn't. I was staying far away from this man. I didn't know who he thought he was, but I wasn't going to stay around and be this man's abuse victim. That was one thing I had never gone through, and I was not about to start. I was so hurt because I really believed he was a good man. It was hard for me to date after my divorce from Antonio, and the one man I trusted end up hurting me too, but worse. Cheating on me was one thing, but putting your hands on me was another. I knew I needed to do a lot of self-evaluation and work on my self-esteem. The reality was, I had no business messing with a married man period. Even though he said he was going through a divorce, I should have gone the other way. I guess this was my karma, because God sure didn't like ugly.

"I won't," I finally said.

"I'll call you," he said, closing my car door. I couldn't get out of there fast enough. I backed out of my parking spot, and part of me wanted to put the car back in drive and run him over. He wasn't even worth it though. I was going to hold my head high, regain my dignity, and move on in my life. As fast as this whirlwind romance began, it was ending, and under the circumstances, I wasn't even mad.

I picked Alicia up from daycare a little early so I could take her home to get her together. Although Antonio and I had our differences, he was still a good father, and I knew she would be happy to see him. It had been a couple of weeks since he last had her, and they were normally inseparable. His new job required him to travel a lot though, so he wasn't able to be around as much as I knew he wanted to. He turned out to be a crappy ass husband, but at least he made up for it in fatherhood.

"Mommy, what's wrong with your eye?" Alicia asked after I picked her up. After Dwayne hit me, I didn't get even bother to look in the mirror to see if he left any marks or bruises. Alicia confirmed things for me though, and now I was embarrassed.

"Nothing, sweetie. Mommy had a little accident," I told her, hoping she didn't want to play twenty questions. I breathed a sigh of relief when she just shrugged her shoulders and didn't say anything else.

"Daddy is coming to get you today, so we have to get you home and get you ready," I told her, hoping to further distract her.

"Yay! I miss Daddy!" she said excitedly.

I got Alicia ready in no time. Meanwhile, I let my hair down and made sure to cover my right eye with it. I hated that my daughter had to see me like this, and I made a promise to myself that she would never have to again. I wanted the best for Alicia, and I had to set an example for her.

Antonio arrived promptly at three o'clock like he said he would. I hollered for Alicia to come on so they could go. I reminded her to grab her favorite teddy bear. She would call me a million times to check on him if she forgot it, and the Lord knew I was not in the mood for that. I laughed to myself just thinking about it.

"You ready to go, pudding?" Antonio asked her.

"Yes, sir!" she said, saluting him.

"That's my girl. Let's roll," he said.

"Can Mommy get a hug and kiss?" I asked her before they walked out the door.

"I love you, Mommy. Be careful so you don't have any more accidents and hurt your other eye," she said.

I cringed when she said that, and Antonio raised his eyebrow. He told her to wait for him in the hallway. "What is she talking about?"

"Nothing. I had a minor accident today. It's OK," I assured him.

He moved my hair out of my face and shook his head when he saw the bruise that had formed. "That didn't come from no damn accident. Look, your personal life is your business, but if you're going to be with someone who likes beating your ass, just don't have that nigga around my daughter."

He walked out after that, and I stood there looking stupid. I wasn't even going to bother to explain that I was done with the person who did this to me. I normally didn't wear makeup, but I had to work the overnight shift tomorrow, and there was no way I was going to work looking like this. I had to find some type of concealer to cover this mark up.

Chapter 4 Morgan

I was so tired of Tyler and just wanted to move on with my life. I had found out some news today that would send anyone on a rampage, but for some reason, I was remaining calm. I was hurt and in disbelief, but I already knew that he had been cheating on me for the longest. Today just confirmed everything, and you would think it would be enough to leave him, but I loved him. I wanted to believe when he said everything would get better, but I guess only time would tell.

"Hey, bae," Tyler spoke when he walked through the door. I rolled my eyes but went ahead and spoke back.

"Hey. What's up?" I replied.

Although I loved this man with my all, there was still a part of me that was fed up and disgusted with him.

"How was your day?" he asked.

"It was cool," I told him.

"Did you cook anything?"

"Nope."

"Well are you gon' cook?"

"Nope."

"Man, Morgan, come on," he said.

"For one, I'm not a man. Two, I'm tired," I told him. I knew I was setting myself up for an argument that could escalate, but that still never stopped me from speaking my mind. I just dealt with the consequences later. I was used to the shit by now. I still hated it though and wanted it to stop, but I guess this was my life. Every day, I hoped things would change, and I figured that if I just kept loving him hard, he would see that I was a good woman and stop hitting me. Once he knew I was having his baby, that should definitely stop the craziness. Otherwise, we didn't have a bad relationship outside of the abuse and selfish sex. We had fun together and that should certainly count for something.

"Can you please fix dinner. Thaw those Salisbury steaks in the microwave you got from Saveway so you can throw them in the oven. Make that homemade gravy too instead of that stuff out the can."

I knew I was pushing it, but this man just didn't understand that I was exhausted. "You sure do have a lot of demands, Tyler. If you want all that, make it yourself.

As a matter of fact, why don't you ever cook for me?"

"Because you're my wife, and it's your job to do the cooking!" he yelled.

"Well let me get a quick nap for about an hour, then I'll cook," I told him, giving in. I thought about it and realized I really didn't feel like getting choked out today.

"By the time you get up, I ain't gon' want it no more," he said with an attitude.

"Then I'll get you some take out when I get up," I said, walking toward the bedroom.

He came up behind me fast and pulled me back by my hair. "I said get in there and make my dinner," he growled in my ear and then bit my cheek hard. I winced out in pain and knew this was about to take a deadly turn, so I just did as he said.

I huffed and puffed, slamming pots and pans around as I fixed his food. Tears streamed down my face because I was fed up. I knew I needed to leave him, but I felt so weak, like I couldn't. I was about to have his baby, and I didn't want to be alone raising a child. I knew I could always have an abortion, but if he found out I did that, he would definitely beat me senseless.

"What the fuck you doing all that crying for?" he asked. I ignored him and kept making his food. He got up in my face, and I braced myself for whatever was coming next. "So you wanna act like you don't hear me!"

"I told you I was tired, and you don't care. You promised to change, but things are still the same." I sobbed.

"Man, shut that shit up! You act like I'm telling you to do something that's gon' kill you. That's why we steady getting into it. You can't do simple shit. Things would be better between us if you stop acting childish and be a good wife. You want me to be a good husband, though, right? That shit goes both ways!" he continued to yell.

"Then maybe you need to find a new wife who wanna put up with this mess. I'm tired of it," I said, walking away from the stove.

I fucked up right there because he tackled me to the floor and sat on top of me. He began choking me, and at this point, I was just ready to give in. I didn't have it in me to put up a fight, so if he killed me, I didn't even care.

Anything had to be better than what he was putting me through. I knew I had false hope, thinking he would change. He was constantly showing me he wasn't going to. He told me anything I wanted to hear just to keep me around. Right as I felt like I was about to slip from consciousness, I remembered I had a reason to live.

"T-the baby," I managed to squeeze out, continuing to gag.

He finally let go when he heard me say that. I peed all over myself and began coughing. He brought me some water and told me to sit up. I was weak as hell, but I did what I was told. I didn't know how long I would be around to take care of my baby, but I was determined to live as long as I could and be the best mother I could be. That meant I had to fight for my life and conjure up the courage to walk away.

"You're pregnant?" he finally asked in disbelief.

I nodded my head. He kept kissing me over and over. He brought me an ice pack like he always did after hurting me, and I put it to my face where he bit me.

Chapter 5 Jade

I exchanged notes with the nurse whose shift I was taking over. She briefed me on everything going on in the emergency room tonight, including a gunshot victim, a patient who thought he was having a heart attack but had acid reflux, and a lady who was having a miscarriage.

"Why isn't she in triage?" I asked my co-worker about the pregnant lady.

"She's only around nine or ten weeks, and they won't accept them in triage until they're at least sixteen weeks," she replied.

"OK. So what's the doctor's plan with her? I thought we normally just sent women home after they miscarry," I said.

"She definitely seems to be in the process of passing the baby because she's bleeding up a river in there. However, on the ultrasound, the baby is still in the uterus. Dr. Shea said he'll watch her for a couple more hours and go ahead and admit her if she doesn't expel the fetus then. There is no heartbeat, and he doesn't want her to get an infection. He plans to do a D&C in the morning if her body won't pass the baby."

"Alrighty then. Is there anything else I need to know?"

"I sent her blood work down about an hour ago. I haven't checked the system to see if the lab uploaded the results yet, so you might want to check on that," she said, grabbing her purse and heading out.

"Thanks for the updates," I told her, yawning.

I pulled up the patient's chart and noticed her name was Morgan Wright. When I looked in the system and read over her blood work results, my heart sank to the pit of my stomach. This poor woman was HIV positive. Her calcium was also a little low, but all of her other results were fine. I worked with HIV positive patients as well as patients who had full-blown AIDS on a regular basis, but I really felt for her. She was losing her baby and had an illness on top of it. I mean, don't get me wrong. There was medication out here to help individuals live longer with the virus, but it was all about what a person could afford. It wasn't my place, but I checked to see what type of insurance she had. When I saw Blue Cross, Blue Shield, I figured she just might be OK then.

She may have already known about her diagnosis, but we were still required to confirm it with them. I took a deep breath and headed to her room to introduce myself and have our discussion. I knocked gently, and when she told me to come in, I exhaled a little more deeply than I intended to.

"Hi, Ms. Wright. I'm your nurse, Jade, and I'm taking over for Cindy this evening."

"It's *Mrs.* Wright. But hello, Jade." She sighed.

I noticed a bruise on her cheek and more bruising around her neck. It made me cringe and think about Dwayne and what he did to me yesterday. Looking at this woman confirmed that I did the right thing by deciding to leave him alone. I refused to end up like her with multiple bruises.

"My apologies, Mrs. Wright. I just wanted to review your treatment plan with you. Dr. Shea wants us to continue monitoring you for a couple of hours before doing another ultrasound. If the fetus does not pass on its own, he wants to admit you and perform a D&C in the morning.

161

Are you familiar with that procedure and what it is?" I asked her.

"Yes, I've heard of it. I know exactly what it is," she replied flatly.

"Well then I'll spare you the details. Once Dr. Shea makes a decision about what he's going to do, he's going to go over it anyway, so I'll just let him do that then."

She shrugged her shoulders, which almost made me hesitant to continue. However, I had a job to do, and I was used to all types of attitudes and personalities by now. I had enough folks roll their eyes and curse me out, that it didn't even faze me anymore.

"I'm not sure if you're aware of not, but it's standard procedure that we have to inform you of your health status. We got your blood work back, and Dr. Shea will be needing to discuss some things with you," I told her.

"If you're referring to my HIV status, I found out this morning at my prenatal visit," she said.

I nodded my head, actually relieved that was one less talk we would have to have. I still felt bad for her though. I definitely understood her attitude right now and would probably be reacting rudely as well if I were getting blow after blow in one day.

"Well, I'll leave you alone for now and I'll be back with Dr. Shea in a few after I make some rounds," I told her. "Do you need—"

I paused when the door flew open and my heart began racing. What the fuck was he doing here? This man was beyond crazy for real and had found me on my job. I was about to scream for security, but I couldn't get anything out. He looked startled when he saw me, but quickly regained his composure.

"D-dwayne, what are you doing here?" I finally managed to ask.

"*Dwayne?*" Mrs. Wright asked confused. "Since when did people start calling you by your middle name?"

Dwayne just stood there looking dumb as hell, and something told me I was in for a rude awakening right now.

"You know him?" I asked Mrs. Wright. It was pretty damn obvious, but I just needed to hear her say it so I would know this asshole wasn't stalking me.

"Yes. Tyler is my husband. How do *you* know him?" she asked, raising her eyebrow.

"I don't," I replied quietly, about to exit the room. I couldn't believe that I was coming face-to-face with this man's wife.

"No, no, hun. Let's not play games here, Nurse Jade. You *do* know him because you just called him by his middle him, which means he told you that. Second, there is something going on more personal than you want to let off because I can tell by your reaction," she said.

I figured there was no point in playing because she was on to us. They were going through a divorce anyway, so I didn't know why she would care. Besides, she was getting her ass beat anyway, so he wasn't worth the fight. She just needed to let this man go because I surely did.

"Dwayne, Tyler, whatever his name is, used to be my boyfriend. I broke up with him yesterday though. He said you two were going through a divorce, so I didn't think there was any harm in dating him."

He just continued to stand there quiet and with a goofy ass look on his face. He didn't say anything, which made me mad for some reason.

"Oh, no, ma'am. You're sadly mistaken. We're not going through a divorce, but we might be now."

"I'm sorry, Mrs. Wright. I only believed what he told me. I didn't mean for any of this to happen. My apologies to you, your children, and your home."

"Children? The only child we would have had is the one I'm miscarrying," she said matter-of-factly.

This fucking liar. I couldn't believe he made the whole thing up. I was glad that I had decided to leave him alone.

"OK. That's enough of this bullshit. I'm going to go request a new nurse," Dwayne finally spoke up.

Mrs. Wright laughed. "Whatever, Tyler. Just go," she said. Surprisingly, he walked out of the room. I just knew he would have flipped out on both of our asses.

"Let me tell you something woman to woman, Nurse Jade. I'm not even mad at you, because you fell for what you were told, and I actually believe you. Unfortunately, you chose the wrong married man to mess with. As you can see, Tyler is a liar, and he has both of us looking silly in the end. Like I said, I went to my first prenatal appointment this morning, and that's when they told me about the HIV. I was going to tell him about being pregnant this evening, but as you can see, things didn't work out that way. He found out right after he beat me. That was the only way I could get him to stop. By then, I was bleeding everywhere, and we ended up here. He told me to tell the doctors I fell, and to keep him from getting in trouble, I did," she said before taking a breath.

"Well, Jade, I'm done protecting him. I'm done believing things will change or get better because it won't. Tyler needs help, and I truly believe that man suffers from multiple personality disorders, but I'm not a psychiatrist, so I don't know. All I ever wanted was for that man to love me with his all, and now everything I suffered for him is killing me. Jade, get yourself checked out. Meanwhile, contact the police and let them know I want to file a police report for the assault today. Tyler has a problem, and I refuse to die at his hands. I've already been given a death sentence earlier, but at least I have a fighting chance if I free myself from him. From the look of all that war paint piled up on your cheek, I'm assuming you've met his wrath too. It's your choice if you want to keep dealing with him while he's in jail, because I'm filing charges. My hope is that you know your worth and move on like I am. No man's love is worth dying for. I just wished I would have realized this sooner."

I didn't say anything but stood there as tears flowed down my face. I was surprised she reacted so calmly, because any other woman would have been ready to fight after meeting the other woman. I admired her strength though, and she was right. I did know my worth, and I felt bad for judging her a few minutes ago. I just leaned forward and hugged her, because I was speechless. Morgan was right. No man's love was worth dying for.

Acknowledgments

I want to thank all of my readers and everyone associated with Major Key Publishing for your continued support. I hope you enjoy reading this love story, and please leave an honest review and feedback for me on Amazon. Check out my Amazon page for other great reads by me at http://www.amazon.com/author/christinafletcher. You can find me on Facebook at www.facebook.com/authoresschristinafletcher/. Also, check out my new website for information on releases, events, and contests alerts at www.authoresschristinafletcher.com. My blog will be coming to my website soon as well!

About the Author

Christina Fletcher was born and raised in St. Louis, Missouri where you'll notice most of her stories are based. She has a master's degree in human services and works as a community support specialist with individuals who have intellectual and developmental disabilities. When she isn't writing, Christina enjoys taking trips, reading, singing, and fishing. Christina is also working on a project to establish her own nonprofit organization. In the meantime, she looks forward to bringing more new and entertaining stories to her readers.

Am I Worth It?

By Cabria

"What time will you be home?" I nervously quizzed over the phone to my so-called boyfriend, Bo.

"Why?" Bo asked with major attitude. "I'll be there when I'll be there," he snarled.

"Well, I mean, you've had the car all day. I have some things I need to take care of," I explained as humbly as possible.

"And like I said, I'll be there when I be there. Now stop calling my fucking phone, Manaya. I got shit to do," Bo spat before disconnecting our call full of tension.

Sighing, I sat on the edge of the bench that was part of my dining room table. With my heart beating rapidly, I attempted to wrap my brain around how I ended up in the position that I was in. My man, Bo, and I use that term loosely, had been riding around all day in my car. My used blue Kia Optima may not have been what was popping to some, but it was all mine. It got me where I needed to go, and I paid for it all by myself.

Glancing at the time on my iPhone, I shook my head upon seeing that it was damn near five in the evening. If Bo was a loving and understanding man, he would have allowed me to explain that I needed to get to the department of utilities to set up a payment arrangement to pay the water bill. I'd been calling these people all day, but for some reason, they weren't answering the phone. I figured going up there would give me better results, especially since I was scheduled for disconnection. At the end of the day though, why did I have to explain any of this to Bo? For one, it was my car, and two, it was not like he was working. So what was he doing that was so important that he had to ride around in my car all day long?

Feeling beyond irritated, I decided to make my way to the kitchen to do what I did whenever I was feeling this way: eat. I was an amazing cook, but since being with Bo this last year, my weight had spiraled out of control with me gaining seventy-five pounds. With my smooth, rich chocolate complexion, thick, shoulder-length hair that I now kept in box braids, and added curves due to my weight gain, I thought I was still beautiful. I could tell that it had affected me health wise, which was why I wanted to lose weight. But I was still a beautiful sister. Bo didn't agree though. He always found some way to say some hurtful things to me.

As I began to prepare my go-to comfort meal of baked macaroni and cheese and fried chicken wings, my phone began to ring. Excitement filled my body as I hoped it was Bo calling to tell me he was on his way. Instead, disappointment set in when I eyed the screen and saw it was my baby sister. As I prepared the batter for my wings, I debated whether or not to slide the button to the right to accept her call.

Gia and I have had our ups and downs like family did, but at the end of the day, we were sisters. With being sisters, she knew when something wasn't right. With the mood I was in, I didn't have the energy to go down that road with her about my domestic issues. Unlike me, Gia was feisty and had no filter whatsoever. She had never hesitated to tell me how she felt about Bo, and she would never stop until I left his "punk ass" as she liked to say.

Seeing that Gia had called multiple times, I decided to take her call. I would feel bad for not answering if my sister needed me.

"Hey, sis," I forced myself to greet her as upbeat as possible.

"What's wrong, sis?" Gia questioned.

As usual, I couldn't get anything over on my baby sis.

"Nothing's wrong. Just tired from work," I partially lied.

The truth was I was tired from working two jobs at a school as a cafeteria worker and at the casino as a bartender. It didn't make sense to me that I had to work so hard when Bo could be helping me. Whenever I thought about it, my soul began to burn.

"Well you wouldn't be tired if that punk ass nigga you have at home would help. It don't make no fucking sense, Manaya. You have a whole nigga, and I mean nigga because he ain't no damn man. A man would never allow his queen to bust her ass the way he does," Gia snapped.

My sister wasn't so much mad at me. She just hated weak women. The fact that I put up with a lot from

Bo made her see me as weak. She didn't love me any less though. Gia just wanted better for me.

"Where is he at anyway?" Gia inquired.

I knew better than to lie to her again because she would already know.

"I don't know," I honestly replied.

"You don't know?" Gia scoffed. "But he's riding around in your car? Manaya, for all you know, he could have a bitch riding around in your car. So what do you mean you don't know? If you don't know, you damn sure need to find out," she lectured.

"Yeah, you're right," I replied.

"That's all you're going to say about that, sis?" Gia quizzed with disbelief in her voice.

The thing was, I'd been having my suspicions about Bo messing with other women. I had learned to keep my feelings and thoughts to myself. What Gia didn't understand though was that she and I were two different people. She was in a happy, healthy, and loving relationship, whereas I was not. Gia was very confident and sure of herself, but I was not. Growing up, I didn't have the best grades in school. Instead of my mother helping and encouraging me, she constantly called me stupid, dumb, and slow. Gia, on the other hand, was an honor roll student, which my mother praised. Gia was the child that she wished she had in me. I didn't blame Gia for our mother favoring her over me. She didn't try to make me feel less than about it either. I'd always said though it was amazing how two people could come from the same DNA but be so completely different. Besides, even though Gia and I were sisters and best friends, there were some things better left unsaid. They said people took secrets to their grave. Well I knew I definitely would.

"Are you listening to me, Manaya?" Gia sassed, interrupting me from my thoughts.

"What did you say, sis?" I asked while placing the macaroni and cheese in the oven.

My mouth watered as I anticipated it being ready thirty minutes from now. Lately, it seemed as if food was the only thing that made me feel happy.

"I said that you need to call his dumb ass now and ask him where he is. You need to tell him that you need him to come home now. You don't need to do no explaining and shit, because it's your car," Gia stated matter of factly.

Hearing my sister talk with so much confidence was hyping me up a little. I avoided confrontation at all costs, but I did need to stop allowing Bo to walk all over me.

"OK. I'm about to call him now," I informed her.

"Good. Call me later and tell me what happened. Plus, I wanted to talk to you about something else. But we can talk about all that later," Gia instructed.

"OK. Talk to you later, sis."

"OK, sis. Love you," Gia said lovingly.

"Love you too," I replied, disconnecting the call.

The way Gia was protective of me, you would think she was my older sister. I hoped that one day I could fulfill my big sister role and be someone she could look up to.

Anticipation swarmed through my body as I tapped the screen on Bo's name. My stomach was in knots as the phone rang and rang until the voicemail came on. Staring at the phone, I decided to call again. Once again, the voicemail answered my call. My intuitions were beginning to become stronger that Bo was out doing things he had no business doing. Feeling some kind of way, I called for the third time. This time, I was sent straight to voicemail. Bo was intentionally ignoring my phone calls which was messed up for two reasons. He had no idea if I was calling for an emergency, and secondly, I paid his phone bill.

Washing my hands, I resumed cooking my meal. Thoughts of what Bo was doing, him having my car, and not answering my calls, consumed me. Along with the encouraging words from Gia, I was prepared to stand up for myself when Bo returned to my home. I contemplated for a second to call his best friend, Wes, who was the total opposite of him. I decided against that and just pumped myself for my showdown with Bo.

***

"Mmm," I moaned as I savored the taste of my macaroni and cheese.

It was sad that the only moaning that escaped my lips was through the pleasure of eating. Bo and I had sex, but it was only to satisfy him. He claimed that he wasn't physically attracted to me any longer because, in his words, my body was not right. So he would engage me in hour long dick sucking sessions and then would finish it off with me laying on my back. I would always feel nothing, physically, mentally, or emotionally when Bo would slide inside of me. It was a wonder how I would even be wet. I guess it would be from all my saliva which coated his dick.

As I bit into my juicy chicken wing, adrenaline rushed through me when I heard the garage door open. I was prepared to give Bo my list of demands. I had never demanded anything in our relationship. I was always easy going and submissive, but as you could see, it had gotten me nowhere. Now it was time to 'boss up' as Gia would say. Enough was enough.

"Bo, it's after seven o'clock. Where were you?" I quizzed firmly as Bo casually entered the dining room area. Setting down shopping bags filled with clothes, he stepped into my personal space.

"Why you kept blowing up my phone?" Bo snarled, ignoring my question.

Swallowing the lump that formed in my throat, the speech I rehearsed for hours began to slowly fade from my mind. As all of Bo's six feet four inches towered over me, nervousness swam throughout me. This was why I feared confrontation, especially from him. I wish I was like Gia.

"Bo, I told you I had things to do. I needed to go pay the water bill," I uttered, looking at his chocolate face.

Swiping his hands across his low-cut fade and down to his beard, he glared at me with furrowed eyebrows.

"And that wasn't something you couldn't pay online?" Bo scoffed. "Don't fucking play games with me, Manaya. You pay all your shit online," he spat.

"I meant I needed to make a payment arrangement," I clarified nervously.

"So which one is it? You had to pay the bill or you needed a payment arrangement? And why your ass need to make a payment arrangement? You can't pay your fucking bills on time?" Bo fired off questions, inching closer to me.

Him questioning me about my finances sent a surge of rage within me. How dare he asked me about anything bill related considering he didn't contribute to the household at all.

"Maybe I would be able to pay my bills on time if I could get some help. At least I was trying. But while you're out doing who knows what, I bust my ass trying to pay these bills. Oh, and I see those bags full of clothes. Is there anything in there for me? As a matter of fact, how did you even pay for it when you don't have a—" I ranted.

"Ahhhhhhh!" I yelped in pain as Bo rained punches onto my head.

While blocking his punches, I ended up stumbling backward and fell to the floor. Intense pain radiated from my head.

"Bitch, don't you ever in your life question me or talk sideways to me like that," Bo blared as he began stomping me on my legs.

My body shook uncontrollably as I laid on the floor balled up in the fetal position. My wails did nothing to halt Bo's shoes from crashing onto my body.

"You stupid ass bitch, blowing up my fucking phone the way you did," Bo growled, standing over me. "The fuck you think you are? You don't run me. I don't give a fuck if it is your car. Your ass can fucking wait, you nothing ass bitch," he continued, delivering one last stomp to my body.

Peering up at him from the floor, I observed the hate he had for me plastered over his face. Why was he even with me, because it was obvious he couldn't stand me? The deeper question was, why was I with him.

Knocking my plate of food off the table, Bo grabbed his bags and headed toward the bedroom that we shared physically. There was no love present in there.

"With your nasty ass food. I don't know how your ass got fat eating that nasty ass shit. Maybe a nigga would want to come home if your bitch ass knew how to cook. At least if you're going to be fat as fuck, you should know how to burn," Bo grumbled from the bedroom.

Hearing his words crushed my soul. Truthfully, it wasn't anything new for Bo to tear me down mentally and physically. It was just each time it affected me in a new way. Heartbroken, I continued to lay on the floor, sobbing. I could no longer live like this because this wasn't living.

Easing myself off the floor, I held my head in agony as I limped down the hall. Entering my bedroom, I observed Bo changing out of his clothes into a red Polo shirt and some jeans. Glancing my way, he shook his head as I stood at the bed. His brown eyes looked lifeless and held no sympathy for his mistreatment of me.

"What you standing there looking like that for?" Bo spat coldly.

Not seeking another beating, I limped into the bathroom. Staring in the mirror, I placed my hands over my mouth to cover the cries that threatened to escape. I knew Bo had beat me badly, but I had no idea that his punches left bruises on my face.

Opening my medicine cabinet in search of something that would relieve my throbbing migraine, an idea popped in my mind. I was tired, beyond tired of everything. Life was a blessing, only it seemed as if I was skating by. With a dead-end job, a no-good man, and nothing else to offer, I was ready to end it all. Just as I was about to execute my plan, Bo came and interrupted me with his presence.

"What you doing in here?" Bo barked as he snatched the bottle of pills from my hand. "I knew your ass was crazy. Go in there and sit your ass down somewhere. I got somewhere to be, and you in here losing your fucking mind. Crazy fat bitch. Do that shit when I'm gone," he yelled in my face.

Hearing his words cut like a knife as everything I'd done for Bo came rushing to the forefront of my mind. Before I knew it, I began pounding my fists into his muscular chest.

"I hate you! I fucking hate you!" I screamed as I continued to beat on his chest while tears cascaded down my cheeks.

Any man who had some type of feeling for his woman would have been moved by my emotions. It was obvious Bo wasn't one who had any love for me whatsoever.

"You fucking bitch!" Bo roared as he grabbed my wrists with pressure. "Your ass ain't learn from getting your ass whooped earlier I see," he barked as he backhanded me on my face.

Falling onto the bed, I leaped up, attempting to fight back. His stature was no match for my five-foot-four frame. Punching me dead in my mouth, I fell back onto the bed while blood dripped from my lip.

"Stop! Bo, please stop!" I wailed as I curled into a ball.

It was as if the more I begged, the more he used my body as a punching bag.

"Oh, now you want me to stop?" Bo blared. "I told your funky ass to sit down, but you're so fucking hardheaded and don't listen," he continued while using my body as a device for torture.

"Bo, please. Why are you doing me like this? All I ever tried to do was love you." I cried while peeking up at him.

My body trembled as he glared at me with a demonic look. Minutes ago, I desired to end my life with pills, but I didn't want to be tortured to death by Bo's hands, which he used as a weapon. Praying that he showed mercy, it appeared my pleas were heard once he ceased hitting me.

Lying next to me, Bo rested his head against the headboard and brushed my braids out my face.

"Stop crying, OK, Manaya? Shhhh. It's going to be OK. You just make me mad sometimes," Bo whispered as he looked down at me.

Surprised by the tiny amount of compassion he was showing me, I slowly lifted my head. Thinking he was about to hold me, I misjudged when he unzipped his jeans and removed his penis from his boxers.

"Shhhh, Manaya. It's OK," Bo said as he lowered my head toward his manhood. "Suck it, Manaya," he ordered while I sobbed.

Afraid of what Bo would do if I refused him, I opened my mouth and began to give him head. Ignoring my cries and the uncontrollable shaking of my body, Bo moaned as I sucked his penis. Grabbing my braids, he pumped his shaft deeply down my throat. Vomit threatened to rush up my throat at the sickness of being low key forced to perform this act.

"Right there, Manaya. You about to make me cum," Bo groaned, surprising me.

It was then I knew Bo was a twisted individual. Normally what would take hours for him to release, only took minutes. It was all because he was gaining pleasure from my pain.

His seeds filled my mouth as I continued to sob. Jumping off the bed, I ran into the bathroom to spit the contents within my mouth into the sink.

"That was the best head I've ever had, Manaya," Bo bragged as he crept behind me.

Avoiding eye contact with him in the mirror, I rinsed my mouth out and grabbed my toothbrush.

"I'm about to head out," Bo informed me, not bothering to apologize to me or even wipe his penis off.

Nodding, I began to brush my teeth and was thankful he was making his exit. It didn't matter that he was taking my car. Bo had abused me many times, but today took the cake. This was the lowest, even for all that he had done to me. Every fiber in me despised Bo, and he needed to be gone.

***

"I'm so sorry. I won't be able to help you with this matter," the property manager informed me. "But just so you know, you're not supposed to have anyone living there who is not on your lease. So technically, you are breaking the terms of your lease," she advised.

"So what does that mean? Are you going to evict me?" I quizzed anxiously.

Working two jobs was still a struggle trying to make ends meet. The last thing I needed was the added stress of finding a place to stay.

"No, I'm not. You've always paid your rent on time and have never had any issues. So I won't evict you for having your boyfriend living with you. But my hands are tied. The law is the law. Unfortunately, in Las Vegas, once you allow someone to reside in your home overnight, you will have to go to the courts to evict them," she informed me.

Defeated, I sighed and thanked Glenda for her time. Rising to my feet, I walked to my car, which I surprisingly had since Bo was with Wes at the moment. Plopping down on the seat, I searched for eviction information. After skimming through the process, I became overwhelmed at what needed to be done. Additionally, I became nervous about Bo receiving the eviction paperwork from me. Most people would wonder why I just didn't call the police on him. Been there, tried that, with no success. Months ago, when Bo slapped me in my mouth, I sneakily went to the bathroom and called the police. When the two male officers arrived, Bo was watching basketball. Instead of them questioning us as their job description requires them to do, one of the officers began talking to Bo about the game. The other officer spoke with me in the kitchen, trying to downplay what occurred. Basically, he chalked it up to a couple's quarrel. It was beyond belief to me that even in the year 2018, police officers were still carrying on like they did in the Tracey Thurman story from the 1980's.

The ringing of my phone interrupted me from my thoughts. Seeing Bo's name flash across my screen made me nauseous. I remembered a time when I would yearn to hear from him. Now I wished he would just disappear.

"Yes," I greeted as I reluctantly answered his call.

"What you mean, *yes*? Oh, I see your mouth want to be on some jazzy shit. You just don't learn from your lessons, huh? But anyway, I don't have time for that right now. I'mma need you to pick me up, and bring some money with you. I need the car," Bo stated coolly.

"Pick you up and bring you money? Bo, I have to get to work, and I don't have any extra money to give," I partially lied. "Can't Wes pick you up?"

"What the fuck you mean, 'Can't Wes pick you up'?" he mocked me. "Manaya, quit playing with me, and get your ass over here!"

"I'm not going to be able to do that," I stated firmly.

"Manaya, when I see your ass, I'mma fuck you up. Quit playing with me and bring your fat—"

Hearing enough of his promises to hurt me, I disconnected the call. Bo began calling me repeatedly, which I allowed the voicemail to answer. Once my text notifications kept chiming away, I felt the temptation to block him. Instead, I allowed his disrespectful texts to come through. All of this would be evidence when I decided to try my luck with the legal system again.

Glancing at myself in the mirror inside my iPhone case, I ensured my makeup was still intact. Since I was about to meet up with Gia, I didn't want to bring any unnecessary attention to myself. My sister would kill Bo literally if she knew he had been beating on me. Gia was all I had that mattered in the world. So losing her to prison was definitely not an option for me.

Placing my car in reverse, I backed out the parking space en route to LoLo's to meet Gia. She said she had some exciting news to share with me. Gia's vibe was always positive and encouraging. I couldn't wait for the day I could come to her with good news.

Turning my phone on silent so that Gia and I wouldn't be interrupted by Bo's continuous calling, I entered LoLo's. My heart warmed upon seeing my sister wave at me along with the smile spread across her cinnamon face. Approaching the booth, she stood to give me a hug. My body flinched from her touch due to the inflictions Bo left upon my body.

"You OK, sis?" Gia questioned with concern.

"Yes, I'm great," I lied effortlessly. "Just a little sore from working out. I started back again," I continued telling untruths.

"Oh, that's great, sis. I am so happy to hear that. I know that will help you with the back pain you said you were having," Gia stated with a smile.

"Yes, it will. So enough about me. What's this exciting news you have to tell me?" I changed the subject.

"Well," Gia said excitedly, grinning while flashing me with a beautiful diamond ring.

"Oh my God!" I covered my mouth. "Is that what I think it is?" I squealed.

"Yes, sis. Robert proposed to me. That's what I wanted to talk to you about the other day," Gia said excitedly.

Before I could reply, the waitress appeared to take our drink order. Since we already knew we wanted the chicken and waffles, we placed our orders. While the waitress complimented Gia on her crochet locs, I began to feel bittersweet emotions. On one hand, I was ecstatic for my baby sister. On the other hand, I felt like shit because she wanted to share her news with me the other day, but we ended up discussing Bo's sorry self. This motivated

194

me to get my life together. I didn't want to be a Debbie Downer, especially with my sister, the only person who truly loved me.

"Gia, I am so happy for you, sis. You truly deserve happiness." I cried tears of joy once she finished conversing with the waitress.

"Thank you, sis. I am so happy. Robert is a great man. And, Manaya, you already know you are my maid of honor. So we have lots to do," Gia teased as she wiped her own tears from her face.

"Yes. Anything you need help with, sis, just let me know," I assured her while wiping the tears which were pouring down my face.

"Manaya, what is that?" Gia questioned firmly while staring at me.

"What is what, sis?" I asked confused.

"This, sis," Gia clarified as she leaned over, touching the side of my face. "What happened to your face?" she asked angrily.

Opening my case, I peered in my mirror and saw that my cover was blown. The makeup which I applied in an attempt to cover my afflictions had been smudged while crying a few moments ago. Ransacking my brain for the perfect lie, I sighed knowing Gia wouldn't believe anything other than the truth.

"Gia." I sighed. "I—"

"Don't 'Gia' me, Manaya!" she said sharply. "Has that nigga been putting his hands on you?" she spat.

"Yes, but—" I attempted to speak.

"Naw, fuck a but," Gia snapped while snatching her iPhone off the table.

"Gia, please stop," I begged as she pressed numbers in her phone.

"No, Manaya. If you're not going to stop this madness, then I am. You're my fucking sister. What would I look like allowing him to beat on you and not do anything about it?" Gia barked.

"That's the thing, Gia. I am doing something about it," I lied. "Whatever you want to do will make it worse," I explained.

"And what are you doing about it, sis?" Gia quizzed, cocking her head to the side.

"I'm getting a restraining order," I stated, feeling guilty for my lies.

"When?" Gia asked firmly.

"As soon as we leave here," I replied.

"Well, shit, we can go do that now. We can eat later," Gia noted.

"No, Gia. This day is about you. We are celebrating you. I can handle it later on my own. I will be alright, trust me," I assured her with pleading eyes.

"How can I be so sure of this, Manaya? I mean, you are my sister. Why didn't you tell me that this was going on? I thought we didn't keep secrets from each other. Manaya, I can't sit by and let that nigga hurt you. I can't lose you, sis." Gia cried.

Once again, I felt like shit. Here it was, my sister wanted to share the news of her engagement with me, and my domestic life had again taken the forefront.

***

After reassuring Gia numerous times that I was heading straight to the police station after our dinner, she was able to slightly relax. After we went our separate ways, I went home. Each time I lied to Gia, I felt horrible. I didn't want to drag her into my nonsense. It was bad enough she finally found out about my secret. I didn't feel like reliving each incident again and having to explain why I didn't have any faith in the criminal justice system.

Reaching my house, I blew out air of relief upon seeing that the lights weren't on in the house. With Bo running the streets, I would be able to take a warm, relaxing bath while enjoying some music. Bo was such a spirit killer, so any time without him was a major blessing. I was just fortunate that he finally stopped calling and texting my phone.

After parking in the garage, I unlocked my door and headed toward the kitchen. Before I could turn on the light switch, I was yanked by my braids with such intense force I was certain some were pulled from my scalp. Yelling, I prayed that one of my neighbors would finally show compassion and call the police. I knew they had to hear all the constant arguing and yelling. Just maybe they would arrest him this time.

"Shut the fuck up!" Bo roared as he dragged me toward the bathroom.

Trembling, I was rattled with terror at what Bo was about to do with my body. Slamming me into the wall and shutting the bathroom door, Bo wrapped his large hands around my throat.

"Yeah, bitch. Now what were you saying earlier? You were popping mad shit, being all fly with your mouth. You ain't got shit to say now, do you?" Bo taunted me while squeezing the life out of me.

Tears welled in my eyes as I focused on each breath I was able to take. My heart began to ache not so much for me, but for my sister. My disobedience to her instructions of going to the police station had fallen upon deaf ears. Even if they didn't want to help me before, at least I could have tried again.

"Oh, you think I'm going to kill you, huh? I ain't about to spend my life locked up behind a sloppy and slow ass bitch like you." Bo hurled insults at me.

Releasing his grip from me, he grabbed my arm and flung me onto the toilet seat.

"Sit your ass down," Bo barked as he turned on the bathtub faucet.

Probabilities flooded my mind as I thought about escaping. All hope was lost when I realized that my car keys were somewhere in the living room or dining room area. Honestly, I wouldn't be able to run out the bathroom without Bo snatching me up and beating the hell out of me.

"Get in the tub," Bo ordered.

Confusion overtook my face as I wondered why he was being nice suddenly. He just had me hemmed against a wall within seconds of death, and now he wanted me to take a bath. Not wanting to spend too much time processing his demand, I quickly removed my clothes and stepped inside the tub of warm water.

Maybe I will get to relax after all, I thought.

My thoughts were quickly erased from my mind as Bo removed his belt from his jeans. Water splashed onto the floor as he began striking me repeatedly with his belt.

"I know you didn't think you were going to get away with all that shit from earlier. I told you to not come sideways out your mouth with me. You do what the fuck I tell you. Got the nerve to be popping your fucking mouth. You lucky a nigga even with your ass. Your ass doesn't comprehend shit. I see why your mama thinks you're slow. You're slow as fuck. I don't even know why I fucked with you in the first place," Bo spat coldly as he continued lashing me.

Each time the belt connected with my skin, I felt as if I was on fire. My skin began to welt and even bleed.

"Bo, please, I'm begging you. Please stop. I'm sorry." I wailed with my hands up in surrender.

"You pathetic ass bitch. Your fat ass needed to wash your ass anyway," Bo snarled as he delivered a jolting punch to my face.

When my head hit the wall, I let out a piercing cry that I felt from the depths of my soul. The abuse was going from bad to worse. I knew if I didn't do something immediately, Gia would be burying me.

***

Sitting on the edge of my bed, I attempted to nurse my wounds with Aquaphor. I had no idea what to put on my stinging body, but that was all that I had at the time. Staring at the mirror in front of me, I wept as I saw the bruises, welts, and cuts. I was beyond tired of wearing makeup to hide my abuse from my coworkers and Gia. Not to mention, I was tired of the pain in my soul from the cruel words Bo always spoke to me. He never spoke life into me. He never said or performed loving acts for me.

When we first met at my main job at the school where I work in the cafeteria, he was a custodian. He would always come by to make conversation. Eventually, it turned into him flirting with me, and I would always cook him something to eat. He constantly praised my cooking while complimenting me on being a beautiful and kind woman. We ended up dating, and he would take me to dinner, concerts, and basically wherever I wanted to within his financial means. They always said good things didn't last, and that was so true with us. The school district ended up having budget cuts. Unfortunately, certain employees lost their jobs. Bo was one of the ones who were laid off.

Initially when it occurred, he was positive and hopeful about finding a new job. Being his woman, I encouraged him daily about how when one door closes, another one opens. Additionally, I updated his resume and even assisted him with his quest in finding another job. After a few months of not finding work, Bo became discouraged. Sure, he was receiving unemployment, but it wasn't what he was used to getting. So me being me, I suggested Bo move in with me until he got back on his feet. He was hesitant at first, but eventually changed his mind once his car was repossessed. Allowing Bo to move in with me was one of the worst decisions of my life. It was like living with my mother all over again as far as the verbal and emotional abuse. Now I was enduring physical abuse to top it off.

The ringing of my doorbell interrupted my trip down memory lane. I prayed it wasn't Gia. She didn't need to see me like this. Not only would she kill Bo, but she would be disappointed I didn't heed her warnings.

Looking out the peephole, I was surprised to see it was Wes. After Bo punched me in my face earlier, he stormed out with my car of course. I just figured he was going out to meet up with Wes.

Cracking the door slightly, I peeked out to let Wes know that Bo wasn't home. Pushing the door open, I became alarmed. Stepping inside, Wes stared at me while my heart beat rapidly.

"He hurt you," Wes said compassionately, sighing as he eyed me.

Dressed in a white tank top and white shorts, the evidence of abuse was apparent. Nodding, my eyes filled with tears of hurt, pain, and embarrassment.

"Don't cry, Manaya," Wes said, comforting as he pulled me into his arms.

Instinctively, I removed myself from his embrace. Wes was always a good guy, but he was Bo's friend. How did I know this wasn't a setup to make it seem as if I was entertaining anything inappropriate with him? I wasn't worried about loyalty. I was worried about my safety until I could figure out what to do about my situation.

"I think you should leave," I stated firmly, looking away from him.

Wes was a handsome man from his smooth, caramel skin, brown eyes, and tall, muscular build. What made Wes even more attractive was his spirit. He was always positive and upbeat which was the total opposite of Bo. I couldn't understand how they were friends.

"Let me help you, Manaya," Wes pleaded.

"Help me for what? Help me how? You can't help me. No one can. Why would you want to help me? He's your friend. Your loyalty lies with him!" I shouted out of frustration.

"He can't be a friend of mine if he would hurt a Black Queen," Wes retorted, pulling me close to him.

Pressing his lips against mine, Wes slowly slipped his tongue inside my mouth. Not feeling an ounce of guilt, I allowed the brief pleasure of being kissed. Bo hadn't kissed me since he wooed me when we first met. It didn't matter because I didn't desire it from him nor his touch.

"I always felt you were too good for him," Wes revealed. "When I saw him earlier, he said he was going to whoop your ass. Something told me he wasn't joking. I don't take shit like that lightly. My mother used to be in a domestic violence situation. How long has this been going on, Manaya?"

Leading me to the loveseat, I revealed to Wes all the emotional, verbal, and physical abuse I had endured from Bo. Wes periodically rubbed his hands over his face as he processed everything I shared with him. By the time I was finished, Wes had his arms wrapped around me, holding me tight. This was the first time in a long time that I felt comforted. Outside of Gia, no one cared for me. This felt peaceful.

"I'm going to be straight with you, Manaya. You aren't staying with Bo anymore. I know this is your place, and I know what you told me about the police and the eviction laws. But as of now, you are done with Bo. Secondly, Manaya, you have to love on yourself. I would never put you down, so please take this out of love. The first time Bo put his hands on you, should have been the last time. You have got to love yourself to the point that you won't allow anyone to disturb your peace or harm your body. You are too beautiful and loving to be mistreated like this. Look at what he has done to your body. Look at what he has done to your heart," Wes lectured as he placed his hand over my heart.

Tears rolled down my face at the beauty of his words. I felt the genuineness radiate from his spirit. Ready for peace, I trusted Wes would help me with this situation. I was willing to do whatever it took.

***

"Gia, I promise I am OK. Just trust me. I know I have been secretive for a while with you, but trust me this time. I will be in touch with you soon. I swear," I promised my sister.

"OK, Manaya. If I don't hear from you within a couple of days I'm calling the police," Gia warned.

"OK. That's fair, sis. But trust me, you will be hearing from me before that. I love you," I said.

"I love you more, big sis," Gia replied before disconnecting the call.

Hearing her call me big sis warmed my heart. It showed me that she loved me and didn't look down on me for my poor decision making in life. When all was said and done, my sister would be extremely proud of me.

"You ready?" Wes quizzed as he placed the last of my belongings in his truck.

Wes informed me that Bo had been laid up with another female since he left the night he whooped me with the belt. He still had my car, and following Wes's instructions, I didn't call or text Bo about it.

They say that out of every cloud there was a silver lining. My rent was late, and I hadn't paid it. When I told Wes about the process to evict Bo, he suggested I get myself evicted. Initially when he told me, I thought it was a horrible idea. It would ruin my credit, and not to mention, I wouldn't have a place to move to. Sure, I could live with Gia, but I didn't want to bring drama to her doorstep. But Wes explained that I would pretend to be evicted. He knew a girl who could draft up fake paperwork. It was not like Bo could or would verify. For one, the rental office wouldn't give out any information to him because he wasn't on the lease. Secondly, Wes said Bo wouldn't verify with the courts because apparently, he had to avoid them at all costs. Seemingly, Bo had some skeletons in his closet that were about to be exposed.

Sliding inside of Wes's truck, I felt one step closer to freedom as we drove en route to the police station. Afterward, I would check into a hotel. Wes paid for me to stay there until the second phase of our plan was initiated and fulfilled. Spending time with Wes was soothing to my soul. He suggested I go back to school to obtain a degree or even open my own restaurant. Wes told me not to believe all the negative things my mother said about me being dumb. He said I was very smart and capable.

After hearing Bo put down my cooking, I was beginning to question my cooking skills. Wes reminded me that my food was amazing, and that was Bo's way of tearing me down. Whatever I desired to do, Wes wanted to assist me. He wanted it to be on my terms though. He didn't want me to be dependent on any man, not even him. He admitted to having feelings for me but wouldn't take it there with me until I was healed and ready to accept love. He vowed to not go anywhere during my process.

"OK. You know what to say, right?" Wes quizzed.

Nodding my head, I entered the police station.

"I need to report an incident and a stolen car," I informed the officer standing at the desk as I lifted my arms riddled with bruises.

"OK, ma'am. Have a seat. Someone will be with you shortly," he stated.

After providing all the necessary information, I was told I would be notified with updates. Exiting the station, I approached Wes's truck. Stepping outside his vehicle, he walked me to the passenger side and opened my door.

"Remember, this is how a queen must be treated," Wes expressed, locking eyes with me.

Then I did something I hadn't done in a long time. I smiled. Returning the smile, Wes walked back to the driver's side. We headed to the hotel as I relayed everything the officer told me along with the paperwork I received.

***

Wes and I were relaxing in the bed at the hotel. Between talking about our lives, laughing, watching TV, and eating, we were having the time of our lives. I liked how I could be myself around Wes. With Bo, I was always on edge. I never knew if he would strike me with his fist or his words. With Wes, his touch and words were comforting. He was a good Black man.

Wes's phone rang, and he retrieved it from the nightstand. Answering the call, my heart stopped as I heard Bo's voice blaring through the phone. Placing the phone on speaker so I could hear clearly, I listened closely with anticipation.

"What was that, man? Slow down; you're talking too fast." Wes feigned concern.

"That bitch Manaya reported her fucking car stolen. So when I was driving it with my girl, I got pulled over. Then she filed a police report for assault," Bo revealed.

Wes glanced at me to see my countenance on my face. My heart sank to hear Bo say that he had a girl and was driving around in my car with her. It wasn't because I wanted him. It was the betrayal. The fact that he used me for a place to stay, for a car to drive, and to have money in his pocket. It was because he abused me when I only sought to help him.

"Oh damn. So where you at now?" Wes quizzed, even though he knew the answer.

"I'm at the fucking police station, man. And the fucked-up part is they found out about my warrants I had in Virginia for child support," Bo ranted. "My ass is going to end up getting sent down there to do some time. Those people in Virginia don't play about child support. Fuck that bitch. If she wouldn't have been up in her feelings about shit, they wouldn't have found me. Fucking bitch," he fussed.

"Well, I mean, it was only a matter of time before they caught up with you. When you lost your job, you stopped paying child support. You were already in arrears," Wes said matter of factly.

"Yo, whose side are you on?" Bo quizzed. "You know what? That doesn't matter. Check it out. I only get one phone call. I'mma need you to call a lawyer for me," Bo said matter of factly.

"A lawyer?" Wes chuckled. "Yeah, man, I got you," he said while looking at me and shaking his head in disbelief.

"Thanks, Wes. I'mma pay you back, man," Bo said, causing me to cover my mouth to stifle my laughs. "But look, I gotta go. I don't know when these people going to transport me to Virginia, but I'll keep you posted. I'm sure you'll have the lawyer ready by then," he continued.

"Yup. Later, man," Wes said as he disconnected the call.

We stared at each other and burst out laughing.

"That nigga is crazy, Manaya. They have pictures of your bruises and the text messages when he threatened you. Plus, his ass is in the arrears for over twenty thousand dollars in child support. He was only working at the school for three months when he got laid off. Before that, his ass wasn't working. He was trying to con his way into a woman's heart, and he found you. Only reason I fucked with Bo was because we were friends since childhood. When that nigga moved away, I don't know what happened to him. When he came back to Vegas, he was a different man. I'm sorry, Manaya, that you had to go through all that you went through with him. But you won't have to worry about him any longer. Even after he does his jail time, he won't be bothering you anymore. Even if he tried to, now that you have the restraining order, with me be your side, he definitely won't fuck with you," Wes expressed.

"Thank you, Wes. Thank you for everything," I said, placing my arms around his neck to hug him.

Ease flowed through my body knowing that Bo would be far away from me.

"Wes, thank you for helping my sister," Gia said with a smile as I gave her a tour of my new apartment. "I don't play when it comes to her," she sassed.

"That's good to know because I don't either," Wes informed her, smiling with his arms wrapped around my waist.

"Oh yeah. I love him for you, sis. He's a good one, Manaya," Gia noted.

"Yes he is. We are taking it slow though. I have a lot to work on," I informed her as I looked back at Wes.

"Yeah, we all do, but I'm not going anywhere," Wes said, winking at me.

"Yes, that's what I like to hear," Gia said excitedly. "So how much time does Bo have?" she inquired.

"He has to do six months for the child support, and with the trial for assaulting me, he can get a few years. Even if he pleads guilty, he will still do some time," I relayed to her.

"Good for his ass," Gia spat. "They need to throw the whole nigga away," she scoffed.

Thankfully, the night Wes came to my home when Bo beat me, he took pictures of my body. All of that would be used as evidence in court. While obtaining the restraining order as well, it all helped when Bo was arrested for driving my car.

I had a long journey ahead of me with healing, but I was thankful for that. Months ago, I yearned for death due to the abuse I endured. So many people didn't make it to see another day due to domestic violence. I was blessed to be able to escape with my body intact and my heart not damaged beyond repair. I wasn't sure of what the future held for me, but I was certain I would love on myself and never allow anyone to break me down in any form or fashion ever again. I knew for sure that I was definitely worth it.

Sins of the Father

By Marcy

Domestic violence is one of the things that no one paid attention to until O.J. Simpson and Nicole Brown. Everyone knows someone, that is being emotionally, physically, or sexually abused.

Skye is someone that has been affected by all three in her life. Skye watched her mother be abused for years. Then after growing up, making it to college, despite the death of her mother and father, she witnesses her best friend, Shay, go through the same things her mother had. The worst thing in the world is to be ignored or abused by the people that you love. After years of watching her best friend's abuse and knowing what her own life turned out to be like without her parents, Skye felt that the best way for her to help her godchildren and Shay was to take the wrap for the murder of Marvin Watson, Shay's husband.

In this story, now Skye contemplates if it was even necessary for her to sacrifice her freedom, because it seems as if nothing has changed in Shay's life. Was she really a hero? With the news of a new man in Shay's life and the bruises on Shay's face, Skye has learned that the "Sins of the Father" are stronger than love and sacrifice.

"Daddy, what are you doing here?" I asked my father who had pulled up in front of my grandparents' house. My mother and I had left him a month earlier. We were visiting my granny and granddaddy because my granny had come home from the hospital.

"Baby, don't you miss me?" he asked me as he got out the car. I was so scared I could feel my heart pounding.

"Come on over here and give your daddy a hug," he said as he walked toward me. I took two steps back. "I said come here, dammit!" he yelled as he barreled toward me with his arms outstretched. He tucked me under his arm and headed toward the car. I wished that I had stayed on the porch where my mother had told me to stay when she walked into the house. I had started to yell and wiggle as much and as hard as I could.

I was six years old, and that was the last day I saw both of my parents alive. My mother and I had been living in a shelter for about a month. We were not supposed to go to a place where my dad could have found us. My mother could not stay away from her parents when she called home and found out that my granny had gotten out of the hospital.

"Momma, Momma!" I shouted as he rounded the trunk of the car.

"Kelvin, Kelvin!" I heard my mother yelling at him. He kept walking as if he never heard her. He didn't stop until the loud sound of the screen door clamored shut. He jerked around quickly and glared toward the porch at my mother coming toward us. "Kelvin, where are you taking her?" my mother inquired calmly. She had learned that yelling back at him just made the situation worse. She was talking to him like a child throwing a tantrum.

"Bitch, you're not taking my baby from me," my dad replied with anger. "Lynn, why did you leave me? I didn't mean to hurt you," he pleaded. It was a stark contrast to how he was acting just a moment before. That was the reason why we left; you never knew who he was going to be from one moment to the next. He could come home from work excited and happy. Then without rhyme or reason, he would be angry and violent. He would start breaking things—plates, doors, walls, but mainly my mother.

My mother lost several jobs because she would call in sick. The day after beating her, he would apologize and tell her to stay home. "No woman of mine has to work. I love you too much for that," he would say. The reason was that she was black and blue, and the bruises couldn't be covered. After calling out time after time, she would be fired from the jobs. This made her dependent on him, which was what he really wanted, for us to be unable to leave.

The last time he was violent, he beat her and me. I yelled his name, asking him to stop hitting her, and then he started on me. He slashed me over my whole small six-year-old body with a thick leather strap. When he threw me to the floor and brought his fist up to hit me, she laid her body on top of mine. She put her back to me and was turned, facing him.

"You're not going to beat my child!" she commanded with more determination than I had ever heard her have with my father before. His face changed as if the features in his face were distorted. My father raised his fist and brought it down on her face. The anger he had for me turned to rage toward her. "Go, Skye! Go to your room and lock the door," she ordered me as he first swung the belt across her body and then he began to punch her.

He yelled and threatened her with every blow. "Who the fuck you talking to? I will kill her if I want to and kill you too!" he bellowed, with every other word. He stopped when he heard her speaking again.

"Not my child. You won't hurt my child," she repeated as she looked him in his eye. "Never will you hit Skye again," my mother added firmly. Her defiance unnerved my father. He dropped the belt and stood still, staring back at her, before he turned on his heels and staggered out of the door.

My mother seemed to be unaffected by the beating she had just taken as she packed our clothes in several bags. When she was done loading them all in the car, she grabbed me, and we left the house.

"We are going to the hospital to make sure you're okay," she said to me as she looked at me in the rearview mirror. Those were the only words that I could understand as she continued to mumble as we drove. When we were in the emergency room, we spoke to a lady that was, as my mother put it, getting us some help. That was the last time I saw my father until now.

"You know why I left, Kelvin. You beat Skye. She didn't do anything to deserve that! That's why," my mother answered, raising her voice. My mother stopped at the bottom of the stairs. She was about ten feet from me, but the fear inside made it look like a mile away. I reached and yelled for her while I was dangling from under his arm. My mother motioned for me to be still and quiet as she spoke to him. "Kelvin, give her to me," she pleaded as she slowly started to walk toward us both.

"No! You don't want to be with me, fine. But you can't take her. She is mine!" he shouted as he turned again to get into the car to leave.

"Give her to me, and I will go with you. Take me, please. I promise I will go. Just put her down, please!" she begged loudly, her voice cracking. My father stopped again and turned back around.

"No you won't. You will just leave again!" he shouted back, sounding like a child throwing a tantrum.

"I promise, I will go with you," my mother replied in a soft tone. She sounded the way she sounded when she was trying to comfort me when I got hurt. "Remember, we promised each other for better or worse," she added. Using the words that he would use with her the day after he would beat her seemed to have gotten his attention. My father started to head back toward her as she walked toward him.

"I was wrong to have left you, Kelvin," she said as they were facing each other on the sidewalk. My mother wrapped her hand around my small arm and pulled at me as she spoke to him. "Come on, Kelvin. Give me the baby so we can go. I promise I will go wherever you want. And we can talk," she said calmly again. He still had not let me go. " I promise... just let the baby go, and we can leave," she pleaded with him, and with that, he released his firm grip from around my stomach. My mother slowly reached under my arms to pull me toward her.

"Yes, we promised that. We are supposed to be together 'til death we do part," he added in the same monstrous tone that was oh so familiar. My mother grabbed me up in her arms and squeezed me. I could barely breathe. She suddenly turned, taking one step toward my grandparents' house.

"Where you going, bitch!" he shouted as he grabbed her by her hair, stopping her. He pulled her close to him. The sudden jerk back made my mother release her tight grip from around my body.

"Nowhere, Kelvin. I'm just putting the baby down," she answered calmly. He let go of the handful of hair he had in his hand. My mother then squatted and set me down. I didn't want to let her go. She peeled my arms from around her neck as she whispered in my ear, "Baby, let momma go. You got to get down." The tone in her voice gave me the sense it would be okay. She had always kept her word. So I unwrapped my arms and legs from around her, and I stood on my feet, facing her. My mother looked me in my eyes and rubbed the tears off my face and kissed me softly on my face before she spoke.

"Baby, go to your granddaddy," she said as she stood and pointed to the porch. My grandfather was standing on the porch, motioning for me to come to him.

"No, Momma. Come wit' me," I whined as I pulled on

her hand for her to walk with me back to my grandfather. My father jerked on her other arm until she was standing against him.. He snatched her hand out of mine and then he stood between her and I.

"Stop it!" he yelled as he lifted his foot and pushed me away from the both of them with it. He kicked me so hard, it caused me to be unsteady, and I fell back onto the sidewalk.

"Girl, gone on and go to your damn granddaddy," he commanded as he yanked my mother toward the car. I didn't move. I was frozen. He turned back toward me. "Go I said! Take your ass to your fucking granddaddy," he added as he was opening the passenger door to the car. It was like he was doing it in slow motion. My mother was thrown into the front seat of the car. My father slammed the door so hard, it made her jerk back as she looked back at me through the window. I was trying to get to my feet.

My mother rolled the window down when she saw me heading for her. "Stop, Skye," she firmly commanded. The seriousness in her voice made me freeze in my steps. "I will be back. Just go back in the house," my mother repeated. "We just going to talk. Momma will be back." My father had walked around the car to get in on the driver's side.

"Go on in the house," my father demanded as he opened the driver's side door. "Do what I say before I beat your ass," he added as he got into the car. The memory of the last beating a few weeks earlier made me grab myself where he had left bruises and turned to walk toward my granddaddy.

"Baby, come on the porch," my grandfather said as he helped me up the stairs of the porch. I heard the car screech away from the curb and peel fast down the street. I watched them drive down the street and turn the corner as if he was late for something. I stopped shy of walking into the house and turned around to sit on the top step. I sat there waiting for them to return for hours. The sun had set, and the crickets were making noise when my granddaddy told me to come in the house. It was still early spring, so the night air was cool. I remember the breeze blowing through my afro-puffs on the top of my head.

I slept on the couch under the big window next to the

front door, all night, waiting for my parents to return. The sound of the doorbell and someone banging on the door loudly was what woke me. I stumbled to my feet and walked over to the door. My mother had returned, and I was happy that she was fine. So happy in fact that I broke the rule of not opening the front door. I was surprised when I opened the big heavy wood door to see two police officers on the other side of it.

"Hey, pretty girl," the male officer said.

"Can I help you?" my grandmother asked the officer as she walked toward the door. "What we tell you about opening the door?" She scolded as she pushed me out of the way. "Go get your granddaddy," she ordered me as she gave me a stern look. Then she turned back toward the two strangers at the door. "What is this about officers?" she asked the uninvited guests.

I walked slowly toward the kitchen so I could hear what they answered. "Do you know Lynn Williams, ma'am?" I heard the female officer reply.

With the officer's reply, I ran to the kitchen where my grandmother had left my grandfather eating breakfast. I slid in the door like Cramer and told him that my granny wanted him. Then I turned back around, running back to my grandmother, leaving grandfather walking slowly toward the living room.

When I got back to the living room, the police officers were sitting down, and my grandmother introduced my grandfather as he walked into the room. "This is my husband, Mr. Smith," my grandmother said as she turned toward my grandfather. "They asking about Lynn."

"What she do? Is she in jail?" my grandfather inquired, not sure why the officers were there.

"No, sir. We wanted to know who she was with yesterday," the male officer replied.

"She left with that jackass of a husband yesterday. I'm not surprised that you would be asking about him, but not my by baby girl, Lynn," my grandfather said.

"But what do you need with her exactly? Is it to press charges on him for beating her?" my grandmother added. She had a little excitement in her voice with the thought of my father being arrested.

"Can you describe what he looks like?" the male

officer requested as he pulled out a small tablet.

My grandfather described what my father looked like and the car that he drove. The officer's movements seem to be in slow-motion as he put the tablet back in his blazer pocket. "According to your description, we believe we found both Mr. and Mrs. Williams early this morning at what the neighbors there said was their home. Gunshots were heard, and the police were called. At the scene they were found dead at what we feel was a murder suicide." Her voice got deeper and the words got slower as they came out of the female officer's mouth.

With this news, I ran out of the house, and I was in the funeral home chapel. Suddenly, I was not young anymore, I was grown, and I saw a closed casket at the end of the aisle in the front of the chapel. As I walked in slow motion toward the front, I saw my grandparents were sitting in the front row with their heads bowed. When I reached the end of the aisle, I stood facing the closed casket. I was never able to see my mom at her funeral, so I had an urge to see my mother's face one more time. I reached slowly to lift the lid to my mother's casket. It seemed to creak as I slowly lifted it with my eyes closed. As the lid was over my head, I took a breath and opened my eyes. I was surprised to see Shay laying there instead of my mother.

"Shay!" I shouted at her, shocked to see her in my mother's casket. Suddenly, she opened her eyes and jerked her head to face me. I jumped back from the casket. Shay sat up and reached for me.

"I'm sorry, I should have listened," she cried to me slowly. Blood started to run out of her eyes. I turned toward my grandparents to see my godchildren sitting there instead.

Suddenly, from behind, my cellmate grabbed me by my shoulders and started to shake me. "Wake up, Skye," my cellmate repeated as she violently shook me. Finally, I opened my eyes to see that I had been dreaming. My cellmate was standing over me.

"Skye, you were having a bad dream again," my cellmate Joan announced. "I would rather you have sleep apnea and snore like a normal person. But instead, you got to scream your ass off with nightmares," Joyce said as she got back on the top bunk.

We were both in this prison for a murder. I sat on the edge of my bed, looking at the newest pictures brought to me by my baby momma. No, I'm not gay like the rest of these bitches in this prison. That is just what I called the mother of my godchildren. One is a boy he's seventeen years old and a girl that is fourteen years old. The boy was named after his father, Marvin, but we called him MJ for Marvin Junior. The girl was named after me. The day Shay told me that she was going to name her after me, I was proud until she told me the whole name.

"Skye, because you have done so much for us, I am going to name her after you," Shay said, beaming with pride.

"Awww, I'm honored," I replied and as I began to give her my middle name. She continued.

"Blue Skye," she added as if she had just named the future president of the United States. I told her with that name, she was setting her up to be a stripper. I could just imagine the DJ saying *'Coming to the stage to brighten up your day, Bluuueeee Skyeeee!'*

Shay and I had been friends since high school, and we

would always be each other's ride-or-die, so she didn't get offended by what I said. Like always, she still did what she wanted to do and named that poor baby Blue Skye. Because she was built like a bag of quarters, she was safe from that pole life, thank God.

Shay and I met our freshman year in high school. We had a lot in common. The main thing was that our parental guardians couldn't care less what we did. Shay was being raised by a single mother that couldn't care less where Shay went and who she was with. I was being raised by my grandfather that had no idea what to do with me. After my mother's death, my grandmother died from a broken heart over my mother's murder. I thanked God every day that I looked like my mother, because I could only imagine what my grandfather would have been like if I had looked like my father.

I didn't think he ignored me because he didn't like me. I thought I just reminded him of what he had lost. When he did talk to me, it was to tell me how not to trust men. *"Don't be like your mother,"* he would say. My grandfather was never involved with my education when I was growing up. He never helped with homework or projects. He didn't go to any PTA meetings or anything like that. But he would constantly demand perfect grades and remind me that I was going to college, and I would finish unlike my mother had done.

Looking at the picture of Blue, I remembered when her mother and I were that age. We were closer than any sisters could ever be. I would give my life for her. People said this, but I mean it. So much so that I was doing life in jail for a murder that I didn't commit. I know what you are thinking as you read this. *They all say that*, but really, this time, it's true. Let me explain.

Shay and I both wanted to leave home as soon as possible. So much so, we made sure that we kept our grades up to go to college. So we were what would have been called nerds. When we got to college, we were totally different people. When Shay and I graduated high school, we went away to college in Tennessee together. Shay and I were two of the finest things on the campus. We were extreme opposites in looks. Shay was short, thin, and light skinned with long wavy hair. Me, on the other hand, I was tall, thick, and dark skinned with short hair. But when we were together, we turned a lot of heads, men and women. When I looked back on our early college years, today you would call us the two of the biggest hoes on campus. We said that we just had a friendly pussy. That behavior was why Shay had children and I don't have any.

Shay and I went to an Omega house party one night that she had been invited to. That night, we both met two Omega Dogs that lived up to their line names. Shay met Marvin Watson, aka Beast, and I met Rick Stone, aka Richie Rich. That night, we got separated, which was against the rule of, *if you come together, you stay together, and you leave together.* I left the party and went up to Rick's room with him. My foolishness back then made me think that his name the frat gave him was true, and it was because he was rich. My momma would say, *"Why will he buy the cow when he can get the milk for free."* So I decided for the first time in my college career, I wasn't going to fuck on the first date. So instead of fucking, we just did some dry humping. We stopped, and I told him that I had to find my friend because it was getting late. But don't forget, I had hoe tendencies. So I wanted to leave him something to think about. Plus, I wanted to see what he was working with.

I pulled down his pants and gave him some head that made him dig his nails into my shoulders. When I stopped, I got up off my knees and said goodnight.

"Girl, you play too much. Where you going?" he asked as I headed out of his room. "You really gonna do a brother like that?" he continued. When I closed the door behind me, I could hear him still cussing. "That's some fucked up shit!" he yelled at me through the door.

I headed for the stairs, smiling. When I got downstairs, I started to look for Shay at the party, but I didn't see her anywhere. I went outside the frat house to see if she was outside on the porch. Shay was neither in the front or the back. I knew I couldn't go back to the house, so I decided that I would just walk back to my dorm. Back then, I was young. My old ass couldn't make that walk now, but it wasn't anything back then to walk a mile or more.

When I had made it halfway to my dorm, I stopped at a convenience store to get me something to drink for the rest of my walk. There were a lot of niggas standing out front of the store. I didn't know if it was more than normal because I was alone or because of there really being more than I had seen before. I walked past them and ignored their "hey babies" and "shorty, what's your name?" I made my mistake when I looked back and smiled when I heard one of them say "Damn, look at that ass, nigga." I didn't know which one said it, but the hoe in me turned and smiled at them all and walked in. I walked around the store, looking for some snacks to take back to my dorm. I decided on some Cool Ranch Doritos and an extra-large Slurpee.

When I got out of the store, all of the guys were gone. I was very glad that I didn't have to hear their tired lines. So I sipped on my drink and headed to my dorm. If I remember correctly, I made it two blocks before they came driving around the corner. They pulled up next to me, but I never stopped walking.

"Where you going, shorty?" the guy on the passenger side asked.

"None of your business," I replied, trying not to look at him.

"She probably one of them stuck up college girls," the one in the driver's seat said.

"I'm not stuck up," I replied. "You don't know nothing about me," I continued.

"Well if you ain't stuck up, get in; we will take you home," someone from the back seat said.

"Naw, I'm good," I said nonchalantly.

"Then fuck you bitch," the passenger said. "Nigga, pull off on this bitch," he added. The car screeched as it pulled away from the curb and turned the corner. I was glad that they were gone.

I thought about the test I had to take in biology Monday as I continued to walk home. I walked in silence for about ten minutes before I heard the engine of a car coming up the street behind me. The car stopped, and when I heard the squeaking of car doors open, I turned around to see two guys getting out of the car, heading my way. It was the guy from the passenger seat and the guy in the back seat.

"Hey, bitch, come here!" the passenger yelled at me.

"Who the fuck you think you calling a bitch!" I yelled back then I turned my back on them both and continued walking.

"Bitch, who you yelling at! You got it all the way fucked up, hoe. These my streets," he added. At that moment, I was mad, which was the first time I ever got angry. I turned, about to face them both.

"Shut the fuck up talking to me. Y'all some bitch ass niggas, and you don't own this street or any other street around here. And you definitely don't own me." I was rolling my neck and waving my cup while I said it to add emphasis. I turned back around to continue my walk, and under my breath, I said, "Fuck boy." When I heard the two doors close back, I smiled to myself. *Girl, you told them niggas,* I thought.

Suddenly, the car passed me and came to a stop. I could only see the driver when I turned back around. "Who you calling a fuck boy?" the passenger asked right before he punched me in the face.

They both grabbed me and dragged me, swinging and fighting to the waiting car that was still running just a few feet ahead of us. I fought them both until the passenger punched me again, and I passed out. When I woke up again, I was somewhere dirty, and one of them was on top of me. I started to fight, and I got punched again. I passed out again. When I came to the second time, I was tied to a bed, and I was gagging. I was gagging because there was a dick in my mouth and someone else on top of me. When I thought to bite down on the dick, a gun was put to my forehead.

"You bite down, I'm going to blow your brains out, trick," the self-proclaimed king of the streets commanded. "Do you understand?" I nodded my head yes. "Good. Now suck daddy's dick," he said as he jammed it down my throat. I looked past him between his legs, and I saw a room full of niggas with their dicks in their hands.

"Niggas, calm down!" he shouted. "Y'all all gonna get some," he said as he waved someone over. "Fuck this bitch," he ordered. Suddenly, I felt someone enter me. This went on for hours, one after the other. When I refused to open my mouth for another dick, he beat me. When I spit the cum out of my mouth, he beat me and had someone fuck me in my ass. After they were done with me, they threatened to kill me if I called the police.

He finally untied me and threw my clothes at me. "Get the fuck dressed," he said. After I got dressed, they took me back to where they snatched me off the street.

"Get the fuck out. Remember, you didn't want a ride home," he said with venom as he got out of the front seat. He reached and pulled me from the back seat of the car and dropped my bruised and battered body on the sidewalk. That was where I laid until I was found by the police.

I dropped out of college and went back home to Michigan. Shay blamed herself for my beating and rape. Later I was told that between the sexually transmitted disease I got from the rape, along with the trauma that left scars on my cervix, it would be impossible for me to have children.

I have to do group anger management sessions. For some reason, the counselor thought that if we wrote out our feelings, it would help me deal with any anger we may have about our incarcerations. The truth was I had never been angry about being in prison until the visit I got from Shay recently. I was here for my godchildren. My godchildren were the closest thing to having my own children I would ever have. So I was going to write about why I had the gun and what really happened for me to be in prison for murder.

Shay had came back home a few months after me with something she couldn't seem to shake either: Marvin Watson. Marvin was all that Shay had after I left, and they started spending a lot of time together. At first, everything was fine, but when she told him that she was pregnant, he got demanding and possessive. Before she had gotten pregnant, they moved in together. He told her they were doing it so he could keep her safe. He convinced her that what happened to me could happen to her if he didn't protect her, so she agreed for them to move in together.

The first six months or so were great. Shay would tell me how he bought her flowers and jewelry. They would go out and spend a lot of time together. But all that beauty stopped when she told him she was pregnant. That was the first time he hit her.

"Who you been fucking behind my back?" he said after he slapped her to the floor.

"Marvin, I have only been with you, baby," she said to

243

him.

"You were a whore when I met you. That's why I invited you to the party to begin with," he said harshly. "Now you trying to trap me," he accused. Shay said he stormed out, and when he didn't come back to the apartment after a week, she decided to come back home to raise her baby. I was glad that she came home because she didn't need to be around him. I could sense that he was a beast.

During her pregnancy, Beast would call Shay, trying to get her to come back. After the baby was born, she sent a picture of his son to him, and two weeks later, he showed up to her momma's house. He had convinced her momma that he wanted to do right by her and his son. Shay's momma all but sold Shay into slavery.

"Shay, it's wrong to keep that man from his son," her mother told her.

"Momma, he hit me then left me. Don't you remember that?" Shay reminded her.

"Shay, he knows he did wrong. He admitted all that. God tells us to forgive and turn the other cheek," her mother said. "I've forgiven him, and you need to too," her mother demanded. I couldn't believe what I heard her mother say. I tried to stay out of family business, but I couldn't.

"So she is supposed to turn the other cheek for him to hit that one too?" I asked, being a smart-ass.

"Why are you still here anyway?" her mother asked me, holding her lips so tight that you could see all the lines around her mouth that were caused from the years of smoking.

I ignored her mother. "Shay, you can get his help without being with him. It's called child support," I said, putting emphasis on child support. "He should be more than willing to pay. He wants to help you raise his son," I added.

"Get the fuck out my house!" Shay's mom yelled at me. "This is family business, not yours," she added as she shooed me out of the house on to the porch. She looked at me through the screen door as she locked it and slammed the other door in my face. I could hear her lock all the locks on the back of the door. "Don't do it, Shay!" I yelled through the door.

I called Shay for two weeks with no response or returned calls. When I would go to her momma's house, she would say she wasn't home. Finally, I got a call from Shay to come over to her new place. When I arrived at the apartment, Marvin opened the door and let me in. I couldn't believe she was with him.

"Where have you been, Shay?" I asked as I grabbed her to hug her. I held her at arm's length to give her a once over to make sure she wasn't hurt. When I saw she was fine, that's when I spoke to Marvin.

"Hello, Marvin," I said, never turning his way.

"Hey, Skye. You rode any trains lately?" Marvin asked and laughed under his breath as he walked out of the room. That statement really made me hate him. I stared at him as he walked out of the room, giving him looks that should have made him drop dead then.

"So where have you been, Shay?" I asked. " Has he hit you?" I badgered.

"No, Skye. He promised he would never do that again," she said. I didn't know if she was trying to convince me or herself.

"It's only a matter of time," I remarked.

"Skye, I called you over here because I wanted to ask you a favor," Shay said with a serious look on her face. "Marvin has asked me to marry him, and I have said yes," she said with a smile.

"So you going to be Beauty and the Beast?" I asked. "So what does that have to do with me?" I added.

"You're my best friend, and I want you to be there," she said with a smile.

"So when is this supposed to be. Next year?" I hoped because it would give her enough time to see the truth about Beast.

"No. We are going to get married in a month. Christmas is coming up, and he wants us to have the same last name. Isn't that sweet, Skye?" she said, shaking me, trying to get me to drink the grape Kool-Aid.

"I don't know anything about planning no wedding, Shay," I said plainly.

"You don't have to. We are going to Vegas!" she shouted.

"So you taking this show on the road, are you?" I stared at her like she had bumped her head.

"Well, maybe you will be excited about who the best man is." Shay paused and stared at me, waiting for me to guess. Instead, I just bucked my eyes at her and waited for her to tell me. "Well guess, Skye." She insisted that I play this guessing game with her.

"Who the fuck is it, Shay! I don't have time for these games!" I shouted.

"Richie Rich! You remember Rick from college?" she asked, thinking that it was good news.

"Shay, there is nothing about that night that I want to remember," I said as I grabbed my heavy purse. The memory of the night made me check my purse to see if my gun was still there. "Shay, I have to go," I said, standing to leave.

"You don't want to see the baby?" she begged.

"I will come back soon since I know where you are now," I said as I walked toward the door.

"I will call you with the details, okay," Shay said as I closed the door behind me.

We all were in Vegas a month later, celebrating the marriage in a club together. The guys went to get drinks, and when they left, a guy approached us and asked her to dance. Shay got nervous and told him no, she was with her husband. She got up from the table and walked away, when the man turned to me. "What about you?" he said reaching his hand out.

"Maybe later. I need to go check on my friend," I said as I got up to find Shay. When I found her, she was in a hallway with Marvin. He had her by her arm and was in her ear. "Hey, is everything okay?" I asked.

"Yeah, it is," Marvin answered. "Ain't it, baby?" he asked, giving the evil eye to Shay.

"Yeah, everything is fine," Shay added, wiping tears from her face.

"Skye, take your friend to the bathroom," he commanded. "Go fix your face," he said, pushing her toward the bathroom. That was the beginning of the end.

After two years of accidents and mishaps, Shay called me because she was ready to leave. I went over to pick her and my G-baby up. When I got there, she was throwing clothes in a suitcase. She had a black eye and a busted lip.

"What the fuck happened to you!" I yelled.

"Here, Skye. Take this suitcase and put the babies' clothes in it." She ignored my question.

I put my purse down and grabbed the suitcase. "I'm not going nowhere until you tell me why you look like that," I demanded.

"We don't have time. Beast will be back soon, and I don't want to be here when he returns," she insisted. "Please, pack everything. The new baby will need it," she added.

"The new baby?" I turned back around and gave her my *what the fuck* face.

"We will talk about it later," she said as she pointed to the babies' room. "Pack, please."

I had only packed one drawer of clothes when I heard the front door slam. "What the fuck are you doing!" I heard Beast yell, slurring his words. He was drunk. *Fuck!* I stopped playing with my godson and started to pack. I could hear Shay pleading with his drunk ass. She asked him to stop.

"Marvin, let go of me. You're hurting me." Shay sounded like a broken record the way she repeated it over and over. I was half done when I heard a crash and what sounded like someone falling.

"Come on, MJ," I said to my godson as I reached for him. "We need to go get mommy."

"So what the fuck you going to do with that?" Beast slurred.

"Get away from me, Marvin. You're not going to hurt my baby," I heard Shay say between sobs.

"I didn't want the first big head bastard. You're not getting fat again," he said. "You can kill it, or I will. Either way, there is not going to be another baby!" he yelled.

"I'm having this baby, Marvin, and I'm having it without you." I was proud that my friend was finally standing up to the beast. As I was headed to the living room to be on her side, Shay screamed, "No, Marvin, stop!"

"Yes, Beast, stop!" I yelled down the hall.

I turned to put my godson back down, and I heard a gunshot. Then Shay screamed again, "Stop, Beast, stop!"

I ran out of the room toward her, and I heard two more

shots. As I rounded the corner into the living room, I saw Shay. She was looking down at Beast bleed out on the floor, holding my gun in her hand.

"Shay, what have you done?" I asked, reaching for my gun.

"He was going to kill my baby, Skye," Shay said in shock.

"Go get your son and leave," I instructed her. I will take care of this.

"Shouldn't we call 9-1-1?" Shay asked, looking at Beast as he reached for her. I kicked his hand away.

"I will call as soon as you leave," I promised. I left Beast dying on the floor while we packed the suitcases and got them into Shay's car. I went back upstairs to the apartment just in time to hear Beast take his last breath. I had to admit I got joy out of it. I picked the phone up like I had promised my friend.

"9-1-1, what is your emergency?" the operator answered.

"I killed a man," I answered.

Fast forward fifteen years later to last week. My best

friend came to see me as she always had since I had been locked up. I sat across the table from her as she was telling me about her momma, work, and her children. Then she began to tell me about the new man in her life.

"See these earrings," Shay said as she turned her head to show them to me. I got distracted by the bruise that I saw on her face next to her ear.

"What the fuck, Shay!" I yelled. "Please don't tell me that I have lost fifteen years of my life for you to end up with another bitch ass nigga that hits you," I angrily added.

"No. My nigga didn't do this, believe me. I would never get in that situation again," she pleaded.

"That's what you used to say about Beast, that he wasn't hitting you," I said. "I guess you fell. No, it was a cabinet. Better yet, the wall moved in front of you," I jested, trying to keep calm.

Shay dropped her head in shame before she responded, "No. None of that. It was Marvin Jr. He did it," Shay answered.

About the Author Marcy

Marcy signed with Major Key Publishing in July 2018. She has been writing most of her life, but after years of doing it for the school, church, skits, spoken word poetry, and her own entertainment, she decided to pursue it professionally. Her stories, though they can be dark and mysterious, she finds the humor in every situation. She has found that her use of humor in any situaion makes anything more palatable. Her *Grace Ford Stories* series will be something that everyone will be able to relate to. She assures that you will be able to relate to more than one of her characters in the series. The first is *Amazing Grace*, and at the time of the release of this anthology, she will be working on the second in the series *Saving Grace*.

Marcy is also going to release her life story *Living Better, Not Bitter.* She shares memorable moments that could have made her life turn the opposite way if she decided to be scared, angry, or bitter. From being molested, almost dying at thirteen, being pregnant at eighteen, and placing that child for adoption, husbands, suicide, and more, she can relate to every woman's struggle, but she chooses to live a better life, not a bitter one by choice.

You can follow her on Facebook, Marcy Douglas Writer, Instagram @marcydouglaswriter. Her website is www.memarcy.com

No More

By Rachal Perez

Hello,

Ladies, my name is Caryne Love, and I want to share my story with you about when loving the wrong man and not loving yourself can lead you down a road of heartache, pain, and maybe even tragedy.

Intro

April 12, 2001

"Shut up, you no good bitch!" Matt yelled at Tiffany as he slapped her, causing her to fall out of the dining room chair. He walked over and stood over and starting beating her.

"No! Please stop, Matt." Tiffany cried out in terror.

Eight-year-old Caryne jumped out her twin bed, ran out her bedroom, and poked her head around the corner. Caryne felt like her heart was going to beat out of her chest from it beating so fast. She watched in horror as her mother got beat up again by her boyfriend. All she could see was her lying on the floor balled in a fetal like position with blood leaking out of her nose and mouth.

Caryne could feel the tears forming up in her big, light brown eyes and fall down her chubby cheeks onto her pink my pony nightgown. She watched as Matt grabbed his black jacket and walked out the back door, slamming it behind him as he left. Caryne could smell the mixture of weed and cigarette smoke as it filled the kitchen. There were empty liquor and beer bottles on the dark wooden table and scattered along the white tile floor. She ran over to her mom and got down her knees.

"Are you okay, Momma?" Caryne asked her mother in a shaken voice.

Tiffany laid on the floor, crying and trembling, shaking her head no.

"No, baby, but momma will be. Can you bring momma a warm towel, please?" Tiffany asked her baby girl.

"Yes, Momma. I'll be right back." Caryne got up from her knees and ran toward the bathroom.

She went into the bathroom and grabbed a white face towel and turned on the water until it was nice and warm and wet the towel like her momma asked her to. When she returned back to the kitchen, her mother was now sitting in the chair, holding her head in her hands.

Caryne walked up to her mother and began wiping blood off her mother's face.

"All I wanted was for someone to just love me. Why wouldn't somebody just love me for once?" Tiffany said to herself.

"I love you, Momma," Caryne said to her momma as she wrapped little arms around her mother's waist.

Caryne felt her mother body start to shake uncontrollably as she held Caryne tight.

"I love you too, my baby. Momma is so sorry you have to witness all of this. Just know, baby, that sometimes, love does hurt. Matt really does love me and you, but he's just been under so much stress. I... never mind, baby; you too young to understand what I'm talking about. Just know that momma is trying, and I love you very much."

Tiffany picked up Caryne and sat her on her lap and held her baby and cried.

Caryne prayed and asked God to please remove Matt out of their lives. She was tired of seeing her mother getting beat up all the time. She wanted a family like all the other kids. She wanted a momma and daddy and a baby sister along with a nice big house and dog. She closed her eyes and held her momma.

November 2008

A young sixteen-year-old Caryne couldn't wait to make it home to tell her mom she made the cheerleading team. She tried calling her mom's cell phone, but it kept going straight to voicemail. She jumped off the yellow school bus and began running home. Caryne froze in her tracks when she made it to her home. She saw all the police cars and people standing in front of the house, then she saw the yellow tape wrapped around the house. She dropped her pink and purple book bag and took off running.

"Mom!" she yelled as she approached the house. That's when she saw the police taking Matt out of the house in handcuffs. She could see the blood all on his white t-shirt and tan shorts. He had scratches all over his face. Matt was tall and dark skinned with long French braids going to the back. Caryne saw a white sheet with blood stains on it, and she could see her mother's lifeless hand.

Caryne felt her head begin to pound and her body shake. She balled up her fists and began pushing people out her way until she got close to him. She started swinging her fists. She hit him with all her might.

"You killed my mom! Why you kill her, you son of a bitch!" Caryne yelled at him.

Matt looked at her with a blank cold stare as they put him in the car.

She felt somebody pick her up by the waist. She couldn't see who it was because the tears were filling her eyes.

"Mom, Mom, please get up. Please. I love you please, Mom, get up." Caryne cried. She was kicking and twisting, trying to free herself from the cop's tight grip he had on her.

"I'm so sorry, baby girl. She's gone. She is gone," the male cop told her.

"No. Just take her to the hospital, please. Mom, come on, please. I love you and need you. Please!"

Caryne let out one loud final scream, and everything went black.

A week later

Caryne sat at her mother's funeral, feeling empty and numb. She had cried so much that she had no more tears left. She had tuned everybody out. She didn't hear the "I'm praying for you," or "sorry for your loss," or the "I love you and here for you" words coming from her mother's friends and family. She just wanted one more conversation with her mom, another hug, another kiss, or to hear "I love you, my baby." Caryne's whole world changed at this very moment because the reality was her mother was dead and not coming back. Matt was charged with rape and second-degree murder. Her and her grandmother Beverly, which was her father's mother, found out that her mother had finally found the courage and strength to leave Matt. She had found a shelter that was willing to help her get away. Matt came home early from work and found her mother packing up their things. He got angry and snapped, and he raped and stabbed her mother forty-three times. The neighbors heard the screaming and called the police.

Caryne was proud of her mother for finally seeing that

she could make it without Matt. Caryne made a promise to herself she would never get mixed up or involved with or love a guy like Matt. She felt the sun shining on her face as she looked up and saw a white mist. For a quick second, she saw an image of her mother's beautiful face with a smile, then the mist vanished.

Caryne closed her eyes and told her mother "I love you."

Chapter 1

July 2, 2015

Caryne woke up from her dream in a cold sweat. She had another dream about her mother. Caryne reached over and grabbed the bottle of water and opened it and took a couple gulps. She grabbed the damp pink face towel and wiped her face off and looked at the black alarm clock on her nightstand; it was 5:15a.m. Caryne pushed the white lace cover back and got up and walked into the bathroom. She used the bathroom, washed her hands and face and brushed her teeth. Caryne walked over to dresser and pulled out a pair of black sweatpants, a white and black Nike shirt, and a pair of all-black Nike running shoes. She got dressed and grabbed her apartment keys and her white head phones and iPhone and walked out the apartment and locked the door, ran down the stairs, and opened the door to the downtown streets of Baltimore, Maryland.

"Damn you fine as hell, baby," the black guy said as he walked past Caryne while she did her stretching before she started her morning run. Caryne was used to all races of men flirting with or complimenting her. Caryne was funny when it came to men and dating. Life had taught her that men could be liars, cruel, and even possible killers. She never allowed a guy to pick her up or come to her house. She always gave them her google number and not her real number. If anything, she learned how to be careful when it came to men and love. Caryne was the spitting image of her mother. She was five feet seven with an athletic curvy figure with a toffee colored complexion. She had long straight black hair that was all hers. She had a round face with round light brown eyes, a slender nose and full lips. She kept her eyebrows and lashes on point as well as her makeup, when she put it on. She looked at her watched and set it for an hour and forty-five minutes to run and fifteen minutes to cool down afterward. Caryne put her headphones in and start running.

A two hours later, Caryne decided to stop by Sidney's coffee shop and get water and a caramel latte for later. She walked in the small, cozy building, filled with its regulars. People were sitting at the small round tables enjoying their coffee, a good fresh Danish, or fruit smoothie. She loved Sidney's because the owner and the employees greeted everyone with a warm smile and great service. She stood in line and waited for her turn. While waiting, she checked her phone for any missed calls or emails or texts.

Caryne had finally made it to the front counter. The smiling female cashier took her order and walked off to make her drink. The cashier came back with her latte and a cold bottle of water.

"Okay, your total is $8.45," the cashier told Caryne.

Caryne reached inside of her pocket to get the money out.

"I got it for the beautiful lady this morning," a deep voice said from behind her. She turned around to thank the gentleman, Caryne was in so awe him of she found herself completely speechless. There were no   words to describe how fine this man was.

Standing in front of her was the finest man she had ever seen in her life.

The man was at least six feet one or six feet two. He had a toffee colored complexion with a handsome chiseled face and a thick neatly trimmed shaped black beard. He had light green eyes with a pair of the sexiest set of lips she had ever seen. He had a muscular build. The dark blue suit fit his frame perfectly, and he smelled good. He had a low-cut fade with waves in it. He handed the cashier a twenty dollar bill and told her to keep the change.

"Thank you," Caryne told him.

"Anytime," he replied with a big, white, dimpled smile.

Caryne grabbed her drinks and began walking toward the door when someone from behind her opened the door for her. She knew it was him because of the cologne.

"Thank you again," she told him.

"You're welcome, again. What is your name, angel?"

"It might be angel."

"Well if it is, I'm a lucky man and blessed then to meet a beautiful angel in person."

Caryne continued walking when she noticed the gentleman was walking with her. She stopped in her tracks and looked up at him.

"What are you doing?"

"I'm walking with an angel."

"Oh my God. You are something."

"Yes, and I can be fun, funny, sweet, and caring if you

give me your number and let me take you out."

Caryne felt a strange feeling; something about him was intriguing.

"All depends if you can afford to take me out. And are you married or got a girlfriend or a couple boos or a special friend?"

"First of all, I can afford to take you anywhere in Baltimore, and no to your questions. No boos or wife or girlfriend."

"Well put my number in your phone, and maybe we can set up a date and time."

"What's your name, angel?"

Caryne gave him her number and told him her name and told him goodbye and to have a good morning.

"By the way, angel, my name is Shane!" he yelled at her.

Caryne gave him the thumb up and kept walking.

Shane watched the beautiful woman walked away. She was so sexy, and she had curves in all the right places. He would definitely make sure he won her over. What Shane Henderson wanted, he damn sure got.

Later that night

Caryne was watching a movie on Netflix when her phone lit up. She looked at the number and smiled; it was the guy from the coffee shop, she assumed, because it was a number she didn't recognize.

"Hello," Caryne said.

"Hello, angel," Shane replied.

"So what's going on with you?"

"Nothing at all, I was just sitting here thinking about you pretty lady."

"Awe, you are so sweet."

"I like the way you gave me a Google number and not your real number."

Caryne burst out laughing.

"Hey, if I were you, sir, I would be happy. Because I could have simply walked away and not gave you my number."

"You right, but I can tell you I'm not crazy or a stalker."

"Yeah, okay."

"Secondly, you couldn't ignore me because you felt the attraction just like I did."

"Attraction? Baby, you are dreaming."

Caryne wasn't going to let him know she felt it too. She had been thinking about him since they met this morning, and that was unusual for her. But something about him captured her attention and imagination.

"I'm not dreaming, baby. I felt it, and it was real. You felt it, but I'll let you believe otherwise."

"I see you are a mess."

"I'm good a mess. So will you please have dinner with me on Friday at 8 p.m.?"

"Sure, but I get to pick the place," Caryne said.

"Okay. Where you want to go?"

"The Rattle Club."

"Damn, you are expensive, but I got it. I'll make sure I book the reservations, and do you drink wine or liquor?"

"I drink wine."

"Got it. Well, I will see you soon. Have a good night."

"You too."

Friday night

Caryne came home smiling and dancing; she hadn't laughed that much in years. Shane was the perfect date and gentleman, and the kiss was awesome. His lips were so soft, and she felt a little wetness in her panties. Shane made her feel alive. The crazy part was they had two dates already set up. Caryne threw herself on the full-size bed and just smiled. Then she thought about her mother and how happy she was at first with Matt, but within a few months, Matt changed. Smiles turned into frowns, and laughter turned into tears and sadness. Caryne checked herself quickly. She had to stay on guard, but how could she when her heart was already willing and wanting to be set free.

Chapter 2

Jan 6, 2017

Caryne couldn't believe it had been two and half years since she'd met Shane, and things with him was still as wonderful as they were in the beginning. She loved the fact he showed and gave her so much attention. He sent flowers to her job and gifts to her house and took her on trips. The lovemaking was off the charts. Caryne never knew sex could be so amazing and that she could cum that many times. She was enjoying Shane and his company. Just maybe he was one of the good guys.

Caryne had lived her life making sure she never made her mother's mistake of loving the wrong man. Shane had never hit her or raised his voice or disrespected her. Shane let it be known to men and to his friends and family that she was his woman, and no disrespect was ever allowed.

Caryne's best friend, Cherry, and some of her co-workers thought Shane was heaven sent too. He came down to the mayor's office and bought lunch for her and all of her co-workers. Shane was a top marketing representative at Kay and Kay agency and made six figures a year. She soon found out Shane knew most of the cops, judges, and attorneys that came through the courthouse.

Life was finally dealing Caryne a beautiful, happy, and loving hand. Caryne even confined in Shane and told him about her mother and her childhood growing up. He held her the entire time while she told him the horrible things Matt did to her mom. Shane proved and showed he loved her, and she loved him too. Caryne couldn't wait to see him tonight for dinner. She thanked God he had finally sent her a good man. Caryne went into her bathroom and ran her bath water. Twenty minutes later, Caryne sat in the tub, feeling relaxed and happy. Tonight, she would see her love. She liked that nickname for him, her *love*. Caryne was in love, and she liked it. No, better than that, she loved it.

Chapter 3

Shane hung up the phone after talking to Caryne. He looked at Kia and grabbed her by the throat.

"Bitch, when I say suck my dick, I mean it. Don't make me beat your ass. I already broke on of your arms; I will break the other one. If you try and go tell, I will kill you. Now drop on your knees and open wide, hoe," Shane said.

Kia dropped on her knees and opened wide. Shane smiled an evil grin and unzipped his pants and pulled his dick out and filled Kia's mouth.

Shane walked into his office bathroom and grabbed the dark blue face towel and washed his dick off and zipped up his zipper. Kia was a pretty thick red bone with blonde hair. She was a hood rat from around the way that was known as the dick whisperer in the hood. Shane couldn't lie; Kia's head game made a nigga almost see God. Shane looked into the mirror and smiled. He had everything and all the hoes and bitches he wanted. He was a successful, wealthy black man with fine looks, a nice dimpled smiled, and a body that men envied, and every woman wanted to explore. Shane learned early in life that women couldn't be trusted; the only thing he trusted was money. Caryne had to be one of the baddest bitches he had ever met. She had it all: looks, the body, and the sex were amazing, and she smart as hell. Soon, he would have Caryne trained. He noticed how guys looked at her, and sometimes he wanted to smack the fuck out of her for dressing sexy and for disrespecting him. He would wait until he had her madly in love with him, then boom; he would have her as his property and under control.

Three months later

April 6, 2017

Caryne Love couldn't believe her luck. After all the bad dates, the players, and the so-called users she finally met her Prince Charming. Shane Henderson was the love of her life, and last night he proved that she was the love of his life. All her co-workers and family told Caryne how lucky she was to get a good man who not only loved her but spoiled her too.

He proposed to her last night at the Winter's restaurant

while they were having dinner. He opened the red heart-shaped box, showing off a four-carat princess diamond cut ring. Caryne looked at her hand, and she felt the tears of joy beginning to form up in her eyes again. This was the best experience of her life. Soon, she would be Mrs. Shane Henderson.

Caryne couldn't wait to tell Cherry the good news. She sent Cherry a text message, telling her to meet her at Sidney's coffee shop for lunch. Within a few seconds, Cherry responded back, telling her she would meet her there. Caryne sent back a smiley face and continued typing up her boss's letter to the mayor.

"Oh my God, girl, this ring. It had to cost a couple of thousands, right?" Cherry asked as she held Caryne's hand.

"Girl, I don't know, but I love it, and I love him," Caryne replied.

Cherry looked at her and smiled.

"I'm happy for you, baby. You deserve a good guy in your life. I hope Shane knows he has a great woman."

"He does. I never had a man that showered me with so

much attention and love. And he lets it be known to all his family and friends that I am I going to be Mrs. Shane."

Cherry loved seeing her best friend happy, but she was a little concerned about the amount of attention Shane was giving her.

"Caryne, I think Shane is cool, don't get me wrong, but sometimes he can be a little controlling and possessive at times too. Remember the pink mini-dress you wore, and that guy said you looked good, and Shane went off and tried to fight the guy?"

"Girl, okay, he gets a little jealous at times, but what dude doesn't?"

"True, but I also noticed you haven't worn that dress anymore either."

"Well, Ms. Nosy, I haven't worn it because my baby said he wants me to only wear it around the house. He texts sometimes and ask me to get sexy for him. You know I love looking good for my boo now."

"Cee-Cee, just be careful, and watch out about that jealous thing. Sometimes people will hide their dark side."

"Chile, don't worry. Shane is a good man."

Cherry just nodded her head. She hoped and prayed for Caryne 's sake she was right. Cherry just had a feeling that Shane was hiding a dark side.

Caryne got in her red 2017 Chevy Impala and turned up her radio. It was Friday and time to party and turn up. She drove up to Shane's job and pulled into the parking lot. She saw him standing by his car, talking to his homeboy Tank. Then her song came on, the Migos "Bad & Boujee".Caryne parked the car next to his and blasted the radio and started dancing in her seat.

A few minutes later, Shane knocked on the driver's side window. Caryne turned the music down and got out the car.

"Hey, bae," Caryne said as she wrapped her arms around Shane's neck.

Shane had a stone expression on his face. He grabbed her arms from around his neck and gripped her arm and dragged her over to the back of building.

"I want to make one thing clear. You are my woman, soon to be my future wife. Don't ever show up to my job with loud ass music and dancing like a hoe," Shane said through clenched teeth.

"First of all, I'm not a h—" Caryne started to say, but then a hand slapped her hard across her face.

"I didn't ask for your opinion. Is that clear?"

Caryne stared at him with shock and fear written all across her face. Did Shane just slap her? What in the hell was wrong with him? Caryne couldn't believe what was happening right now. Shane had never raised his hand or voice to her.

"Let me go, Shane." Caryne cried as she tried to break free. Shane closed his eyes and leaned her up against the wall.

"I'm sorry, baby. I just lost it for a minute. You looking all good, and Tank was staring at you and... I'm sorry, baby. Please forgive me."

"No, Shane. Let me go, I will not go through this."

"I'm sorry, baby. I promise it won't ever happen again. Please."

Shane kissed her forehead and then the right side of her face where he slapped her. She felt his dick pressing up against her.

"Damn, Caryne. I love you, woman. I need you so bad, baby. Let me eat that pussy right here," Shane told her.

"Shane, we are outside; anyone can walk up and see us."

"There is no cameras over here. I told Tank to keep watch. I'm going to eat you now." Shane leaned down and started kissing and touching her body. Caryne felt him lift her blue dress up and put her body up against the building and put her legs on his broad shoulders. He reached between her legs and ripped her panties off and put his long tongue inside of her wetness.

Caryne closed her eyes and bit her bottom lip. One damn thing for sure, Shane's head game was the best. She wrapped her legs around his head and let him take her to ecstasy.

Later that night, Caryne laid in the bed, staring up at the ceiling, thinking about what happened earlier. Shane apologize to her over and over while making love to her. He promised to work on his temper and jealousy issues.

Caryne knew Shane grew up in a dysfunctional home, but she did too. His mother left him at the age of four, and his dad died of a drug overdose, leaving him to be raised by his grandmother. Shane was one of the best marketing representatives at Kay and Kay agency in Baltimore, Maryland. Caryne knew if she showed him the right amount of love and care, Shane would be alright. They both would be alright and have a great future ahead of them. Caryne knew two things: she loved Shane, and he loved her. The truth was, if Shane was going to be like Matt, he would have showed it earlier in the relationship. She believed that Shane was really sorry for slapping her. , Sometimes even a good man could have a bad day or go through rough times, especially when you were a young and successful black man. She knew this storm was finally over, and now there was nothing but good and happy days waiting ahead of them.

Love would see them through.

Chapter 4

Six months later.

Oct 24, 2017

Cherry glanced over and looked at her best friend, Caryne, slumped over in the passenger seat. She shook her head and wondered when she would see that her nigga was no good. Caryne's left eye was black, and her nose had dried blood on it. She hated seeing her friend like this. She wanted to kill Shane's punk ass.

Cherry pulled up to her house and cut off the car. She got out and walked around to the passenger's side of the car and opened the door.

"Caryne, wake up," Cherry told her.

Caryne woke up and looked up at Cherry. Her head was pounding, and she could hardly breathe out of her nose due to the dried-up blood. Her left eye was swollen shut, and her right side was in pain from him kicking and stomping her with his boots.

"Okay," Caryne replied as Cherry helped her out the car and into the house. Cherry took her to the guest bedroom, and Caryne laid down on the full-size bed.

Cherry stood over her with her hands on her curvy hips.

"Caryne, I love you dearly, boo but I don't know how much longer I can stand back and keep watching this shit happen. I mean, damn, girl. He fucked yo' face up."

Caryne let out a deep breath. She was so tired of everybody having an opinion about her relationship and her life. First Cherry, then her aunts and cousins. She couldn't get them to understand that Shane's job was very stressful, and she wasn't making things better by being very needy and clingy. This morning, she woke up late and didn't have his breakfast cooked on time. Caryne knew better, but she was tired from staying up all last night, sexing him and giving him head.

Shane called her lazy and stupid. She tried to apologize to him. She even got on her knees and begged him, but he still ended up hitting her. After the beating, he told her if she would just listen and stop irritating him, he wouldn't have to hit her. She loved Shane, and she knew deep down he was a really good man, and he loved her in his own special way.

"Damn, Cherry. I don't need a got damn sermon, okay!

Hell, Shane has a lot of stress on him. And I have to find a way to stop doing stupid stuff that gets him upset. He is very good man deep down. He pays all the bills, and he takes care of me. This is my life, not yours. I'm sick and tired of everybody trying to run my life. This is my life," Caryne replied.

Cherry tilted her head to the side and rolled her eyes. She knew at this point, Caryne was gone.

"You right; it is your life. But it's also interrupting my life too. I get tired of picking yo' ass up and seeing you fucked up or getting phone calls from you crying over this sorry piece of shit. I'm sorry, but I don't have any respect for a man who puts his hands on women or children. So tonight, I have made my decision too. I'm no longer picking you up. If you like getting your ass beat and called out your name, stay there and deal with it, and don't call for help. So you're welcome to stay or leave, but either way, I'm done too. So on that note, good night. Oh, and one more thing. You're starting to look and sound like your mother. Remember and think on that," Cherry told her as she stormed off down the hall to her bedroom, slamming the door.

Caryne looked up to the ceiling and said a small quick prayer. She would leave first thing in the morning. She heard her phone vibrating, and she reached inside of her purse and pulled it out. She had ten missed calls and nine text messages, all from Shane.

Once again, he was apologizing for everything, telling her he loved her, begging her to please come home.

Caryne couldn't help it; she loved him. She texted him back and told him she was at Cherry's house and she would meet him at the corner.

Caryne knew Cherry was right, but she loved her man. She had faith that Shane would go back to being the man he once was. Caryne grabbed her purse, got up from the bed, walked out the room, and left the house.

Cherry heard the backdoor open and close.

"Ooh, why, why!" Cherry yelled.

Martin woke up and rolled over and looked at Cherry.

"Baby, you gotta let her see for herself. Now you have done everything you could. She has to wake up, and she has to be the one to be tired of that bullshit," Martin told her as he rubbed his wife's back.

"I'm so scared I'm going to get that phone call, and it's the police saying she is dead."

"Just pray for her, baby."

Cherry prayed God helped her friend soon.

Once again, Caryne was laying under Shane's naked body. She felt numb at this point. All the arguments and beatings were starting to take its toll on Caryne. She was thinking about filling the tub up with water and drowning herself. Shane made her quit her job so she could be available to him twenty-four-seven.

She found herself depending on him for everything. If someone would have told Caryne years ago she would be in her mother's shoes, she would have laughed in their face and cussed them out. She understood now why it was so hard for her mother to leave Matt. When you were in love with someone, you were blind to so many things. Now here she was in love and being controlled by a man just like Matt.

Caryne tried to fight Shane back one time, and he hit

her so hard her bladder released, and she had pee running down her leg, and she blacked out. When she woke up, Shane walked over to her and kneeled down and got into her face and threatened to kill her if she ever told on him. He let her know that, he could make her ass disappear so fast that nobody would ever find her body.

The look in his eyes were cold and deadly, and he had an evil sly grin on his face. Caryne knew then he was the devil himself. She didn't see any way of getting out of this situation. Just when she thought she broke the cycle, life was proving her wrong. She was reliving her mother's life all over again, and that meant death would soon come her way. Caryne was open to death. She was depressed, broken, and emotionally, mentally, and physically drained. She realized she was once again alone. No friends, no close family... she had no one. She was at his mercy.

The next morning

Caryne had the driver to pull up to the H&S store. She needed her coffee fix. Earl, the driver, opened the car door and helped her get out. She could smell the fresh brewed coffee from outside. The coffee was soothing and comforting to her soul. She opened the door and walked in, noticing the cashier was watching her as she shopped. There was something mysterious and sexy about him. He was a handsome dark-skinned man. Caryne got her coffee and a few other items and walked up to the counter.

"Good morning, ma'am. Is this all?" he asked in a deep baritone voice.

Caryne nodded her head yes. She made sure not to talk to men because Shane could pop up on her anywhere. The gentleman looked at her with a curious expression on his face.

"Okay, your amount is fourteen dollars even," he told her.

Caryne pulled out her card, slid it through the terminal, and hit credit and then the accept button for the amount. The gentleman tore the piece of paper and give her a copy.

"Are you okay, Ms. Lady?"

Caryne nodded her head again.

"Is someone hurting you? Just nod your head, and I

will call the police for help."

"No! Please don't call no police, sir. I'm fine. I got into a car accident, and my face hit the steering wheel. No one is abusing me. I'm okay."

"Alright. I was just concerned, ma'am. I hope you get better soon."

Caryne grabbed her things and left. Hasan watched the mysterious lady leave. She was a regular customer who came in every week or every other week for coffee. He couldn't help but notice a slight bruising around the lady's eye. He hoped the lady was telling the truth. He hated seeing women and children being abused.

Hasan watched her get into the black car and pull off. Caryne let out a deep breath as soon as she got inside of the car. She was so happy she was quick with an answer. If Shane saw the police at their house, he would be outraged. Caryne had been working hard on keeping Shane happy so he wouldn't go off. All that mattered now was that she loved Shane, and he loved her. Truth was, no couple was perfect.

She tried calling Cherry, but each time, her calls went

unanswered. Caryne shook her head. Clearly, Cherry wasn't her real friend anyway. Shane was right; he was the only person that really loved her and was down for her. Fuck Cherry. She was jealous anyway because her man couldn't afford shit like Shane. Females were haters now a days when you and your man were winning or happy. Shane made her happy, and that was all that mattered.

Caryne looked at Cherry's number and deleted it out of her phone. The hell with it. She grew up without many friends anyway. Caryne decided she would do what she wanted to do, and wasn't no bitch, man, or whore going to turn her away from her man.

291

Chapter 5

Four months later

Feb 2018

Hasan Reed unlocked the front door to the H&S store. He knew the kids from the neighborhood would be coming in soon. He looked at his Longines Stainless Steel Hydro Conquest watch. It was 6 a.m. on the dot. He walked back to the counter and set up the different flavors of muffins and fruit cups and bottles of waters.

Hasan heard the doorbell ring as the door opened.

"Hey, Hasan, what's good?" Demery asked.

"I'm good, and you, little god?" Hasan replied as Demery walked up to the counter and grabbed a muffin and a water. Demery was a young dark-skinned, skinny kid with short locs. He was one of the happiest kids he had ever known. Demery was always smiling.

Hasan liked him because he was a great kid and very smart. They both shared a common interest in sports, cars, and comic books.

"I'm straight. Just nervous about this math test I have

to take in fifth hour today."

"Hey, you going to do just fine. Just remember the steps I showed you. Trust me; you will ace it."

"Okay. I'll let you know."

"Alright."

Hasan heard a loud commotion coming from outside. Someone was screaming and yelling.

"Stay right here, Demery."

"Okay."

Hasan walked toward the front door and opened it. He saw to his left a couple that was arguing and fighting right in front of Mr. Lee's hair store.

"You stupid fuckin' bitch!" the man yelled at the woman as he slapped her across the face. The hit caused the woman to fall down onto the ground. The man then grabbed her hair and starting punching her in the face and kicking her.

Hasan ran over toward the couple and grabbed the man by his shirt and pulled him off the woman.

The man looked at Hasan with his fists balled up.

"Get the fuck off me, nigga," the man growled.

"I'm not on your ass yet, nigga. How about you gone on and walk away and leave the lady alone," Hasan replied.

"I don't have to do shit, muthafucka. You all in my fuckin' business. I suggest if you don't want to get fucked up or die, take your ass on."

Hasan narrowed his dark brown eyes at the man. Little did he know, he could kill him in less than ten seconds without a weapon. But he noticed out the corner of his eye Demery was standing in the doorway watching him.

"Well that leaves me no choice but to call the police," Hasan told him.

"Please don't call," the woman said as she slightly lifted up her head.

Hasan looked down at the battered woman and frowned. She had a big purple and blue bruise on her face and a bloody nose and a busted bottom lip. Then he recognized the lady; she was one of his regular customers that came into his store to buy coffee.

The man walked around Hasan, reached down, and grabbed the woman by her upper arm and yanked her up.

"See, I can't take your trifling hoe ass nowhere. Wait until we get home," he told her through clenched teeth as they starting walking away.

Hasan began following behind the couple. He had a really bad feeling that if the woman didn't get away, she could possibly end up being killed by the man. The man turned around and pulled out a gun and aimed at him. Hasan put his hands up and stopped.

"Back up before I put a bullet in between your eyes; this is my last warning. Who are you, captain save-a-hoe?"

"Naw, I just don't want to see nobody dying tonight, man."

"The only person who will die is you if you keep following us."

Hasan nodded his head.

The man put the gun back under his white t-shirt and continued walking.

Hasan watched the couple until they disappeared.

"I wish I had a gun. I would blast that fool," Demery said while standing behind Hasan.

Hasan turned around and looked at Demery.

"Listen to me. A gun comes with power and problems. Yes, you can get respect, or end up in prison. That punk ass, bitch ass nigga is no man. Real men don't put their hands on women. A man's job is to protect is his woman or wife and his family and friends. Come on; your bus will be coming soon. I better not see or hear about you carrying a gun. If so, you and I are going round for round in a boxing ring," Hasan told him.

Demery's eyes grew wide.

"I won't. I promise."

"Good. You got the smarts to make it to Princeton and I'm going to make sure you make it."

"Yup. I'm going to be either the best heart surgeon or defense attorney in the country."

Hasan pulled Demery to him and hugged him.

"Yes you will. Come on, man," Hasan replied.

A few minutes later, the school bus came and picked up Demery.

Hasan walked back into the store and stood behind the counter. He pulled out his iPhone and pulled up the security cameras. He watched the video and saw that the couple stopped by a black Lexus with tinted windows. The man grabbed the woman by her head and banged it up against the car and opened the car door and shoved her inside then slammed the door, walked around, got into the car, and took off.

Hasan put the phone down and shook his head. He would have killed the sorry piece of shit if Demery wasn't watching. He had two pistols on him as well. He just didn't understand why women stayed in relationships with men like that.

He would look over the tapes later and get the license plate number so he could get more information on dude. Payback was a must; nobody pulled a gun on him and not suffer the consequences.

Chapter 6

Caryne Love couldn't keep her focus because she kept going in and out consciousness throughout the car ride. She was praying that Shane didn't shoot the store guy. She didn't want to see nobody getting killed. Once the car stopped, Shane opened the car door and pulled her out. Shane unlocked the back door to the house and pushed her inside.

"Take your messy ass inside of the bathroom and wash your ass. While you in there, put on some that Bath and Body Works shit. After that, lay your ass down on the bed. I feel like fucking tonight. And fix your face too," Shane told her as he sat down at the kitchen table and began pouring the dark liquor into the shot glass.

Caryne nodded her head and walked slowly to the bathroom and began to take her bloody clothes off. She left the bathroom door open so Shane could see her. Shane didn't like for her to close any doors in the house. He wanted to have eyes on her at all times. He had security cameras throughout the entire house. She could only leave when he went out to places.

All her phone calls were monitored and recorded. Everybody thought that Shane was the man because he worked for Vincent Vines. Vincent Vines was a well-known underground drug lord. He covered his tracks by buying up businesses and stores and using them for fronts. Most people looked up to him like Robin Hood because he took care of those in the ghettos or in the hood. Shane's job was to make sure all the cops, attorneys, and judges got paid very handsomely so Vincent could continue his dirty work.

Caryne couldn't bring herself to look into the mirror. Because all she would end up doing was just shedding tears and pissing off Shane even more. An hour later, after soaking in the tub, Caryne got out and dried herself off with the towel and moisturized her body with the Hello fragrance from Bath and Body Works and fixed her face using a small compact mirror.

She let her long black hair down and walked out and laid naked on the king size bed.

Shane came in and stood at the foot of the bed. He

climbed in the bed and started kissing her. Once upon a time, his kisses made her head swim with desire; now, she feared him completely. The kisses made her sick to her stomach.

She watched him as he took his finger and stroked her face. Shane loved Caryne, but sometimes she made him mad by acting stupid.

Shane wanted her, and he went after her with everything he had. Money, trips, dates, and even mind-blowing sex. He had to make her his and control her too. She would be his until he got tired of her ass. Right now, he couldn't and wouldn't let her go.

"Caryne, I'm sorry, baby. I just got so mad; you know I love you, right?" Shane asked her.

"Yes," Caryne replied in a whisper like voice.

"Good. Just know I love you so much I will kill someone over you. You mine, and you will always be mine."

Shane gripped her chin and made her look into his eyes as his other hand wrapped tightly around her throat.

"If you ever think about leaving me or going to the cops, I want you to know I will kill you. Nobody will ever find you. I have power over the cops and judges. I run Maryland. Do you understand?"

"Yes, I do."

Shane leaned down and kissed her on the forehead and then her lips.

"My good girl."

Caryne just closed her eyes and let Shane have his way with her body. After they were done, Shane rolled off her like it was the best. She hadn't even cum; she hadn't cum in months. She learned to moan and scream at the right moments so he thought he was really satisfying her. He pulled her close to his body.

"My good girl; my property," he said as he went to sleep, leaving Caryne with a million thoughts running through her head. Why? Why? Why?

She closed her eyes and cried silently to herself.

Chapter 7

Hasan sat in his office at home and began researching the videos and the plate number. He found out the dude's name was Shane Henderson, and he lived in the west side of Kingstown. For him to stay over there told Hasan he had money. He needed Cotton and Rage to help him. He grabbed his office phone and called up Rage.

Ring, Ring

"What's good, bro?" Rage asked in Haitian accent.

"Hey, bro. I'm good, and you?" Hasan asked him.

"I'm good; smoking some good kush and rubbing on my wife's big, round, soft ass."

"I need a favor."

"Alright, name it."

"I need information on a guy named Shane Henderson; he stays in Kingstown on the west side. He drives a black Lexus with the plate number GHU8899."

"What the deal with this one?"

"He pulled a guy on me earlier."

"Wait, and this nigga ain't dead?"

"I couldn't; little god was watching, so I had to remain cool. Trust me, he would have been on Channel 3 local news at noon today."

"So how the situation lead to a gun being pulled?"

"He was beating on a woman."

"Oh shit, Hasan."

"Rage, I don't need a lecture. Are you in or not?"

Rage let out a deep breath.

"Yes, my brother; we blood brothers 'til the end."

"Blood brothers 'til the end. I'll send a little gift so you can take Cotton shopping."

"She would love that, but you know I take care of my woman."

"I know, but you know if I eat good, my whole team eat good too."

"Real shit there. I'll be there in a week. Your old man got me on a job; once I'm done with that, we will be there."

"Cool."

"You talk to your pops?"

"Yeah. His ass at the strip club looking at new girls."

"Pops a pimp."

Hasan burst out laughing.

"Yeah, so he thinks. Hey, after mom died, he suffered a deep depression. So to see him out and about enjoying life is all good."

"True. Well, I gotta go; my baby is giving me the eye. I will talk to you later."

"Yup."

Hasan ended the call and put the phone down and looked out the window. He loved living out in the woods. It took him two and half hours to get to the store every day. Growing up with his father, he had grown tired of the fast city living. He took more after his mother. She loved the outdoors, nature, and the ocean. She told him if he ever wanted to have peace, move by the water or out in the woods. Hasan looked at the beautiful woman's picture in the picture frame.

"I told you I will always keep my promise. I am, and I love you always," Hasan said.

He got up from the chair and turned off the computer. He needed to get in bed early tonight. The supply trucks would be coming in the morning, and he had to have all the paperwork done as well. Hasan walked over and turned the lights off. He took a long, hot shower and dried off and pulled the covers back. He heard his phone beeping, so he picked it up and saw seven text messages from Shana, Raye, and Tasty. He just wanted to be alone tonight; he wasn't deep stroking anybody. Maybe tomorrow night he would see what was up. Hasan put the phone down and turned off the small table light and went to sleep.

A week and half later.

Caryne had finally sweet-talked Shane into letting her go run a few errands by herself. She had been doing everything he wanted her to do. She cooked, cleaned, gave him sex and head, however and whenever he wanted it. He let her go with a driver/babysitter, of course. The driver was an old black man named Earl. Little did Shane know, Earl liked Caryne, so he let her enjoy her outing and he never told Shane a bad report.

Caryne try to put on a enough MAC makeup to cover

up the bruise on the left side of her face. She grabbed the black Gucci shades and put them on .She put a blonde colored lace front wig on hoping that the clerk wouldn't recognize her. Caryne let out a deep breath and got out of the black Lincoln and went inside.

Hasan saw the lady enter the store and head toward the third aisle. He smiled to himself. The woman really thought that a wig and big black shades would keep her from being recognized. She looked good in the black fitted dress, showing off her thick, curvy shape and nice toned legs along with the red bottom heels and red purse. She was sexy as hell. He had a small crush on her for a while now, not knowing she was with a jerk.

He watched her as she grabbed the three bags of Hollow's Coffee. He kept the coffee in stock because so many people loved the taste of it. He knew the coffee was on the high end, but he knew the CEO personally, so he got it for free. He brewed the coffee every morning for the customers and for some of the homeless people as well.

Caryne felt the butterflies in her stomach. It was something about the way the cashier stared at her that gave her that exciting feeling. It felt like he could see right through her, all the way to her soul, and see all of her secret desires that she longed for.

He was a very handsome man, but she was sure a man like that was either taken, married, or a player. Caryne shook her head. Why was she fantasizing about this man? She had enough men problems as it was.

She continued walking up slowly toward the counter, placing the coffee on the counter.

"Good morning, ma'am. Is this all for you today?" Hasan asked her.

Caryne nodded her head and reached inside of her red Gucci purse and pulled out her wallet and the cash. Hasan bagged up the coffee and handed it to her. She passed him the money.

"No. It's on the house, beautiful."

"I'd rather pay, sir," Caryne replied.

"I'm not taking your money. It's on the house."

"Okay. Thank you, sir.

"You welcome, and remember you are too beautiful and too good for him. Real men don't beat on women."

Caryne grabbed the bag and started walking toward the door.

"Excuse me. I have one question to ask you."

Caryne froze instantly. *Not that question, please.*

"Why do you stay with him? I mean, the makeup looks good, but it don't cover up the bruise all that well. I can still see the dark colors."

Caryne turned around fast and looked at the man. He was taller than Shane, standing around six feet two, with a stocky, muscular build, a dark skin complexion, and a smooth bald head with a trimmed shaped beard. He had dark brown eyes with long eyelashes that women would kill to have. His lips were nice and full. They looked so soft, and Caryne shook her head and looked at him and smiled.

"First of all, let's be clear. My man is good to me, and he loves me very much."

"You love him? So he got you believing that love comes with fists to the face? What is it going to take for you to kill him, or he kills you first?"

"Sir, I don't have to explain shit to you or anyone else.

Have a nice day."

Caryne started to walk away.

"I'm sure you practice that speech every day in the mirror. Caryne Love, and your man is Shane Henderson. Y'all live in a nice townhouse in Kingstown. The happy couple."

"How do you know my name and my man's name? Do you know who my man is? Trust me, he is not the one for the games," Caryne asked him.

Hasan looked at her and gave her a big, huge smile and walked up to her and whispered in her ear.

"I'm not either. Have a good day, beautiful. See you again soon. You smell like heaven. If you were my woman, you would smile every day, trust me. I would never hurt you."

"Well point is, I'm not."

"You right—you not. But maybe I have to change that and take you from him."

They stared each other down for a few seconds before Caryne broke eye contact first and turned and walked out like hell itself was on her heels. She got in the back of the car and told Earl to take her the mall. Her heart was beating fast, and she was so turned on. She could still smell his cologne and feel his breath on her skin. She had to make sure she bought another pair of black lace thongs. She was wet just from him being near her.

Caryne had found out Shane didn't have any cameras in the closet. She had a little toy bullet that looked like lipstick. She would often go in the closet and quickly use it to release and imagine it was the store clerk. She gave him the name chocolate Prince because he was so handsome and dark.

Caryne hurried and got herself together. Shane would kill them both and would kill her if he knew her thoughts. She lost count on how many times he had cheated on her.

Caryne's phone started ringing, and she looked at it and saw Shane's name on the screen. She pushed the accept button to video chat with him.

"Hello, how are you?" Shane asked her.

"I'm good. Just out shopping. I'll be home shortly."

"Enjoy and take your time. You been a very good girl lately. I was wondering if you can pick up something sexy and wear it for me tonight."

"Sure, what color?"

"Red or black."

"Okay. I will buy both colors."

"Good. I see that last ass whooping got you right, huh?"

"Yes it did. It's my job to keep you happy, bae."

Shane smiled at her.

"Love it. See you soon. Love you."

"I love you too."

Shane blew a kiss and ended the video chat. Caryne put the phone down, and just like that, all her happy thoughts were gone. She thought back on when she met Shane. He was her prince charming, the perfect gentleman. He was so sweet and kind, funny and fun. She met him at a coffee shop.

Their romance was like a whirlwind type of romance. He wined and dined her and bought her gifts and took her shopping and took her on trips. All her co-workers and friends often called her lucky for getting such a great catch. The first year was so amazing that by the second year, he proposed to her, and she said yes. He told her she didn't have to work, and he wanted her to be an at-home wife and mother. Well, within a couple months after she said yes, Shane changed.

His attitude went from nice to nasty. He would call her a cheater and a liar. One night after an argument, he got so mad, he grabbed her and starting choking her. When she got free from him she left him for a week after that, but he begged and promised her he wouldn't do it again. He promised he would get counseling and take anger management class, but he never did. He ran all of her friends off because when she would go to their house to get away from him, he would show up and act up. It got so bad to the point all of her friends moved or changed their numbers and blocked her on social media.

No women's shelter would take her in because he threatened the people. She had nowhere to go. She was left alone, and he had her right where he wanted her: alone and depending on him. She thought loving him would help. She just wanted her best friend and the man she fell in love with back. She would see him the old Shane at times, the man she fell in love with but then the evil side would show up and take over. She loved him very much, but she didn't know how much more abuse could she take? Or would she wait too late and end up dead?

Chapter 8

Hasan knew she felt the attraction between them. If she was single, he would have made her his by now. She made his manhood get hard just by looking at him. He wanted to kiss those sexy ass lips. He was tempted to say fuck it and put the closed for lunch sign on the door and take her to the back and lift the dress up and lick and eat her from front to back and stroke her so deep. Damn, he had to wait. He had a plan in motion, and he meant his words; she would be seeing him very soon.

His phone beeped with a text from Rage, telling him he was on his way to the store, and he had some news for him.

Twenty minutes later.

Hasan looked at the pictures then back at Rage. Rage was five feet ten with a slender muscular build with a dark skin complexion with long black locs that hung down his back. He had hazel colored eyes with a nicely trimmed goatee.

"Yeah, deep. I know. I had the same look on my face,"

Rage told him.

"Wow, and he thinks he is the man?" Hasan asked him.

"Yup, running around town like he got big balls because who he works for."

"Well it's time for a different plan. Let's show him and his boss who we work for as well."

"So what's up with this woman? You got a thing for her?" Rage asked.

"Something like that. I been feeling for her a minute; I just never worked up the nerve to ask her about her status until I saw him beating the fuck out of her. I wanna kill this nigga for real."

"Just say the word."

"Meet me back tonight around 10 p.m., when the store closes," Hasan told Rage.

"I'll be here."

"Yup. See you soon."

Rage gave him a dap and left.

Hasan had a huge smile on his face. He was going to enjoy taking Shane's woman and seeing how tough he was with a gun pointed in his face. They didn't call him No

Mercy for no reason.

Chapter 9

"Please, Shane, baby. You hurting me." Caryne cried as he twisted her wrist.

He was drunk as hell and on one of his rampages again.

"I'm going to ask you again, who else you fucking?" Shane asked.

"Nobody."

"Lies. All you women are liars. You know my mother was a liar like you and my ex-wife. I killed my ex-wife, and the cops believed it was suicide. Cops are so stupid. With the right amount money, the law will overlook a lot, even murder. Tonight, I'm going to get away with it again."

Caryne looked into his eyes; they had a different look about them. They had no life to them, just a blank, cold stare. Caryne thought about the statement the cashier asked her earlier today. *Either you going to kill him, or he is going to kill you.* All she could she see was her body lying in the casket. Tonight, right at this moment, death was in the air, and it was coming for her.

She heard a faint voice that sounded like her mother.

"Get out now before you die," the voice said.

She had to get out this car one way or another. Shane was driving pretty fast. Before she could do anything, he back slapped her in the face. He hit her so hard she saw stars.

"You not going anywhere. You hear me?"

For a few seconds, Caryne's vision was blurry, but she had to fight this time. She reached over and grabbed the steering wheel and turned it to the right. The car ended up hitting a parked car, and everything went black.

Caryne woke up to hearing a horn blowing. She saw Shane was knocked out with a bump on his forehead. She undid her seatbelt and opened her door. She heard him moaning. She had to go now.

With her vision still blurry, she got out, and her right leg gave out. Blood was trickling down on the right side of her face, and her side was hurting. Caryne began limping away. She kept pushing herself until she thought she was far away from the accident. Caryne stop and prayed.

"Please God, help me. I have no one, nowhere to go, and I need protection. Your child needs you. Please, Father," Caryne said, then she blacked out again.

Caryne woke up and looked around. She was in a big soft bed, but whose bed? Where was she? She had on a blue t-shirt. Her heart started to race. That meant Shane or his goons had found her, and he was going to kill her.

"Relax, you're safe," the voice said. She turned her head and looked into a pair of the sexiest dark brown eyes. It was him.

"Where am I? How did I end up here?" Caryne asked him.

"You passed out in front of my store last night. Now the question is, what happened to you?" he asked her.

He had his arms folded across his chest. The man was sexy as sin. He had on a white wife beater with a pair of dark blue sweatpants. He had huge, muscular arms with tattoos that covered both arms, and he had some on his chest. She noticed he had on a silver bracelet. She saw the name Asia on it. Must be a girlfriend or maybe his child.

"I was in a car accident," she replied.

"What happened? Somebody hit you, or were you drunk?"

"No."

"Hmm. I got a good guess what happened. How is your head feeling?"

"Okay, but still a little sore."

"Me and my brother found you last night in front of my store. I thought you were dead at first. We did a pulse check and found one, but you still needed medical attention. We put you in the car and took you to a friend of ours that is an E.R. doctor. He told us you had a sprained ankle and a nasty bump on your head. My sister-in-law, Katina, but we call her Cotton, is a registered nurse. She checked your vitals out and cleaned you up. The doctor gave you some pain medicine, and now you're up, sunshine."

Caryne looked around the bedroom. The big open window showed beautiful greens trees with big white clouds and blue clear skies. The bedroom was decorated with light wooden furniture. She felt like she was in a log cabin.

"Where is Shane?"

"In his skin; he alright. He a little paranoid 'cause he can't find you."

"What you mean? Shane knows everyone in Maryland... cops, judges, attorneys."

"Yeah, but he don't know me. Trust me, he will know me soon."

"What is your name?"

"My name is Hasan."

"Hasan."

He liked the way his name rolled off her tongue. He peeped that she was looking at his bracelet. Hasan sat on the edge of the chair and pulled out a yellow folder and passed it to her. Caryne grabbed it and opened it. There was a picture of a beautiful woman holding acute little girl. The next set of pictures were of burned up bodies. Caryne looked at him.

"That's my baby sister. Her name was Asia, and that is her daughter, Harmony. Five years ago, my sister's boyfriend killed her and my three-year-old niece because he found out she was leaving him. She called me and told me to hurry and come get her. She was ready to come back home. She lived in Los Angeles with him. I told her I would be there in two and half hours. But by time my plane landed and I made it to her place, she was gone. We looked for her and my niece and her boyfriend for four days straight.

The next day, we found her missing car. He had set the car on fire with them in it. He had killed her and the baby with a single gunshot to the head. He tried to hide, but I found him, and I spared him no mercy. So this bracelet is made out of her and my niece's favorite jewelry pieces. It's a reminder of them. I'm telling you this because I couldn't save them, but I will do my best to save you if you want to be free of him and happy."

Caryne felt a tear roll down her face. The hurt expression on his face while telling the story broke her down. It was such a sad story.

"Caryne, do you want to be free, or do you want to go back to him?" Hasan asked her.

"No. I want to be free and start a new life."

"Good. Now focus on healing; I got you."

"Thank you, Hasan. But where will I go? I have no family here or friends anymore due to Shane."

"You have me now, beautiful."

"Why do you call me that? You know my name."

"Yes I do, but I like calling you that. Trust me, you are safe now. You will never have to worry about anything again. No one will harm you. This is the next chapter of your new life. "

Hasan reached down and grabbed her hand and then lifted it to his lips. He kissed the inside of her hand as Caryne held her breath. His lips were soft just like she imagined. After that, he got up from the chair and left out the room.

Caryne sat in the bed and closed her eyes and said a quick 'thank you' prayer to God. She was now safe and away from Shane and his abusive and controlling ways. Caryne had a very strong feeling that Hasan meant each word.

Hasan went down to the kitchen and walked out the back door. He pulled out his phone and called his dad.

Ring, Ring.

"Well hello, my son. How are you today?" his pops asked.

Hasan could tell from his father's voice he was happy that he had called.

"I'm great, and you, old man?" Hasan replied.

"Living the dream, son, and looking at beautiful women."

"I'm calling to tell you that I will be attending this month's business meeting with you. I think it's time for me to reintroduce myself again."

"Oh really now?"

"Yeah. When is the next meeting?"

"In two weeks. Do I need to throw a party?" his father inquired.

"No, not at all. I just ask that you let me lead this one."

"You know I will; you are my right hand. I trust you with my life."

"Okay, Pops. I will see you soon, and don't get in trouble with the ladies now," Hasan said.

"Never that."

"Love you."

"I love you too."

Hasan smiled; his plan was set.

Two weeks later.

Shane felt like shit. It had been almost four weeks and still no sign of Caryne. He woke up in the hospital with minor bruises and a bump on the head. He had all of the cops on payroll looking for her, but nobody had seen her. When he got her back, he would teach her a very serious lesson. Nobody left him.

Shane sat at the table with all the top men who helped run Mr. Vines' daily operations.

Mr. Vines walked in dressed up in a black suit with a black and white silk tie and black dress shoes. He looked well to be just sixty years old, but you couldn't let the age fool you. Mr. Vines could be a ruthless coldblooded killer. He was respected and feared at the same time.

Mr. Vines sat down at the end of the big table.

"Good evening, everyone. Tonight, there is going to be a change in the meeting. I have someone here that I would love for you all to meet. I'm sure you all have heard about the guy called No Mercy, Mark, bring in our special guest, would you?"

Mark got up and opened the door, and within a few seconds, a tall gentleman walked in.

Shane felt like someone had slapped the shit out him. This was the same dude he pulled a gun on when him and Caryne were fighting. He heard of the No Mercy guy; he was legend. He was a known, trained killer who never missed a target. When he got rid of a body, it stayed buried, never to be found again.

"Everyone, this is my son, Hasan, better known as No Mercy," Mr. Vines told everyone.

Everyone gasped in shock. Shane was in total disbelief. He'd been knowing Mr. Vines for ten years now and never knew he had a son. He only knew about Asia.

Hasan zeroed in on Shane and smiled.

"Well, everyone, my name is Hasan, and I am Mr. Vines' only son. I took a leave of absence from the operations long time ago. I'm back now, so there will be some new changes happening, starting now. Oh, but before we start, I have a secret guest as well. Beautiful, come in," Hasan said.

Caryne came in and stood next to Hasan.

"Shane Henderson, you, sir, will get the gift of a lifetime tonight. Beautiful, do you have any last words that you would like to say to Shane?" Hasan asked as he walked over and stood next to Shane and stared at him with a smile.

"Shane, you made my life a living hell. You beat me, you took away my life, and my family and friends. You made me feel worthless and unattractive. You are the devil itself. I hope you suffer for all the pain you caused me. I want to show everyone here what Shane really does when you guys are not around," Caryne said.

Caryne grabbed her phone and connected to the computer and walked over and pulled the screen down for the projector. She pushed play videos of Shane beating her and beating up other women as well.

"Oh, but that is not all. Mr. Vines, you're going to love this," Caryne said with a smile.

A video popped up showing Shane pulling a gun out

on Hasan. Mr. Vines looked at Shane with a stone expression on his face.

"Everyone out, now! Black and Red, y'all stay. We got a problem, Houston!" Mr. Vines shouted.

Shane was nervous. He knew what the price was when it came to Mr. Vines being betrayed. Hasan pulled out a gun on Shane and put it to his head.

"You not so tough now, are you?" Hasan asked him.

Shane closed his eyes and took a deep swallow.

"I didn't know. I'm sorry," Shane replied while shaking like a leaf.

"I don't accept apologies from cowards or bitch ass niggas who beat women," Hasan told him.

"Shane, Shane... you disappointed me, son. I thought you were better than that. I take it very personal when my son or family is threatened. You picked the wrong one to pull a gun on. He could have killed you even with the gun in your hand. I'm going to really miss you, but oh well," Mr. Vines told him.

Hasan pulled the gun back.

"You know what? I got a better idea for you. Sit yo'

ass down," Hasan told him.

Shane sat down in the chair.

"Put your hands on the table," Hasan told him.

Shane put his trembling hands on the table. Hasan walked over to the wall and grabbed the sword and walked over to Shane. Hasan leaned down and whispered in his ear.

"I'm going allow you to be my spokesperson to show I can have a little mercy."

Hasan raised the sword and cut his left arm off and then walked over and cut his right arm off.

Shane sat in the chair, screaming, in pain and in shock. Hasan took his foot and kicked the chair with Shane in it and watched it hit the floor. He took another swing, slicing off his feet.

"Black, come get this piece of shit and take him to the hospital, and if he talks too much, kill him," Hasan told him.

"You got it, boss," Black told him as he grabbed Shane by the lower leg and dragged his bloody body out.

Hasan took the black rag and wiped the blade off and

gave it to Red.

"Clean it off. Tell any of the men if we find out they are abusing their kids or wives, they will be looking just like Shane; if not, they will be dead," Hasan told Red.

"You got it. I will pass it along," Red replied.

Mr. Vines burst out laughing.

"You still ruthless," Mr. Vines said to his son.

"Only when need be. That punk ass nigga beat her like a dude on the street. All I saw was Asia, and I just wanted to save her since I couldn't save my baby sister and her baby. That haunts me to this day," Hasan replied.

"Me too. I love her and my granddaughter so much. I miss them. I just wished she didn't hide the signs of abuse. I would have killed that bastard sooner."

"Right. That part. I got to go and check on beautiful."

"You mean your wife?"

"I didn't say all that, Dad."

"You didn't have to. I see it in your eyes."

Hasan walked out the building and got inside of the black limousine where Caryne was sitting in the back, waiting on him.

"Is he dead?" Caryne asked him.

"No, but you best believe he won't punch or kick another woman a day in his life," Hasan replied.

Caryne slide over and kissed Hasan.

"I always wanted to do that to you."

"You ready to live a happy life?"

"Yes. Will it involve you in it?"

". Yes, it will."

"Thank you, Hasan."

Hasan grabbed Caryne's face tenderly and continued kissing her.

A few months later

Caryne couldn't believe how much her life had changed. She was now working at the store with Hasan and going to school to be a counselor so she could help other women who suffered from abuse. Shane was wheelchair bound and shipped back to his family so they could take care of him. All the women didn't want anything to do with him.

Hasan made sure she was safe, and he kept his word. He never raised his voice or hand to her. He treated her like a queen. In the end, he saved her life, and she saved his. He even proposed to her, buying a beautiful seven-carat ring. He claimed he had to let the world know she was taken. Hasan made her get rid of her toy. He said his mouth and dick would keep her satisfied every night, and he wasn't lying about that. He was a great lover. Caryne had even connected back with old friends and family members. Demery had even come to like her too and called momma dukes.

Life was good, and Caryne was free and happy. Love now came with hugs and kisses from her bae.

Domestic violence (also called intimate partner violence (IPV), domestic abuse or relationship abuse) is a pattern of behaviors used by one partner to maintain power and control over another partner in an intimate relationship.

Domestic violence does not discriminate. Anyone of any race, age, sexual orientation, religion or gender can be a victim – or perpetrator – of domestic violence. It can happen to people who are married, living together or who are dating. It affects people of all socioeconomic backgrounds and education levels.

For those who have been affected by relationship abuse, those who are currently in abusive relationships, and those who are working to heal, call the National Domestic Violence Hotline:
1-800-799-7233

Be sure to LIKE our Major Key
Publishing page on Facebook!

Printed in Great Britain
by Amazon

20141018R00190